Blood Feud
Moira Kane

ISBN (eBook Edition) 978-1-7350097-3

ISBN (paperback edition) 978-1-7350097-7-3

ABOUT BLOOD FEUD

A LEGACY BUILT ON *a lie.*

Sophia is a bored and lonely princess, more content to live out her days locked away in her chambers than facing the increasingly grotesque suitors her father forces on her. With her younger brother destined for the throne, there isn't much value to her but in a marriage alliance. And so, she is destined to live out her days as the trophy wife of some fat merchant or lecherous lord, occasionally bearing children to bolster the ranks of the wealthy and powerful.

But trouble is brewing in the crumbling streets of Calos. While the future king sits pretty on his throne and dines on fancy foods, there are whispers of rebellion among the poor and downtrodden people. At the same time a dragon has taken up residence in Calos Valley—the first in fifty years.

With no valiant hero like her famous grandfather, Saint George the dragon slayer, Sophia's father turns to the old way to ward off the beast—a maiden sacrifice. What better choice than the daughter that threatens her brother's reign?

Sophia is no trembling damsel, however, and the dragon is not at all who—or what—he appears to be.

CHAPTER 1

SOPHIA

"Sacrifice? What do you mean I'm to be sacrificed?" Sophia spun away from the window and narrowed her eyes at her father.

"You're to *make* a sacrifice." Father ducked his gaze and made some meaningless gesture with his bejeweled hand. "For your family and your kingdom."

"I won't marry some disgusting old man only to be a broodmare, Father." She stomped the heel of her bare foot on the cold stone, sending a painful jolt up her calf.

It was a petulant move, but it was no more childish than her father's scattered muttering and refusal to meet her gaze. He was a *king*, for Gods' sake. Not a king of much these days, thanks to the fire breathing fiend that was turning the kingdom of Calos into his personal banquet hall, but the man with the furthest reach and the greatest power within four days' ride should have more guts than that.

Then again, this was the same man who was being cowed by a reptile.

"Come again, daughter?" The king hissed.

She examined her nails and blandly repeated. "*I said*, you're being cowed by a reptile."

"A reptile? Is that what you would call that monster darkening our skies and thinning our already dwindling herds?"

The dragon could hardly be blamed for dwindling herds. Sheep were already too gaunt after a long winter, the cows not producing enough milk. It was only the latest problem Calos was suffering through—the *people* of Calos were suffering through. Sophia and her family knew nothing of suffering. Her father was blind to it, only making note of the growing poverty when it was due to his mismanagement of gold and poor trade choices.

No, that was still false. Even when Calos fell deeper into debt and the shepherds were as rail thin as their sheep, Father took no responsibility. So long as he could host extravagant feasts and boast about his family history of heroics—heroics that he took no part in—he cared not for the status of the royal coffers.

There must be a shortage of pork steaks and fat pheasants on his table if he was hovering in her bed chamber, letting her know that he'd once again made a match for her with some fat pocketed merchant or wealthy lord from across the oceans. As if that would save his kingdom.

"It has scales and a pointy face. It's a reptile."

"It's a *dragon*."

"Yes, and? Don't you have brave knights ready to prove themselves by slaying it and saving us all?" The words tasted sardonic in her mouth, but she could tell by the ruddiness collaring his throat and brightening his sagging cheeks that he was taking her seriously.

"My knights are not equipped for such a fight."

"And why not?" She made a slow lap around her chamber, finger tapping her chin thoughtfully. "Surely a *dragon*," She smirked privately as she whirled to take another lap. "Is no more difficult to kill than a lion or a bear. The knights of Calos have lengthy experience killing both."

"A bear?" Father sputtered. "It's maw alone is the size of a bear!" The redness was climbing from his jaw to his forehead, painting his pale face with anger. "Enough of this! You are shifting the subject because you wish to make me forget my task. Is it any wonder you've gone this long as an unmarried maiden? No man wants a wife with a tongue that bites sharper than his sword."

"Yes, yes, I'm quite terrible." This conversation was deader than a horse and she had no interest in watching her father beat it again.

The last time he tried to broach the topic, Sophia got a good laugh by insisting that she wasn't a maiden at all. Unfortunately for the guard that was often assigned to follow her when she was briefly allowed outside the castle walls, Father had sought to punish whoever dared touch the princess of Calos. She tried to spare the man a flogging and admitted her lie, only to watch him be beaten regardless as punishment for *her*. A just king, indeed.

"What about George?"

"What about your brother?"

"Is he not named for my grandfather, the mighty dragon slayer? Send him out to tame and maim the beast." Sophia had always thought *George Saint George* to be a ridiculous name, but her brother was rather proud of it, wearing the palindrome like a strutting peacock, as if he was Saint George reincarnate and had any claim to their ancestor's heroic deed.

"I came here as a courtesy, *daughter*," His mouth twisted like he was uttering a curse or speaking of some slimy creature rather than his own flesh and blood. "Not that you deserve it."

"The only courtesy you ever did me, *father*, was to spill your seed in my mother's royal treasury."

Every visible inch of the king's skin was flushed the color of a lovely summer wine. Unfortunately, he wasn't heady or sweet. "If your mother—Gods rest her soul—wasn't such a pious woman, I would have thought you born on the wrong side of the bed."

"If only." Sophia flicked her fingers impatiently in her father's direction. "I've been warned, your highness. Now be gone with you. I must prepare to be sacrificed to whatever ancient foreign king has agreed to take my hand to seal the trade contract you're settling this week."

Father sputtered at Sophia's back as she returned to gazing out the window. When he realized he had nothing intelligible to say—and that he no longer had the attention of his audience—he left in a huff, fancy dress shoes clacking on stone. She always thought those stupid shoes to be rather womanly. Most fashion in the high court was. Maybe her father selected her a groom from some faraway northern island and she would be expected to wear nothing but shaggy furs.

If she was particularly lucky, her betrothed would be a barbarian king who wore bones in his hair and war paint during dinner. He might not make the gentlest lover, but at least he wouldn't expect her to be some giggling, brainless twit who flounced around in fluffy pink dresses and blushed under his gaze.

Rosemary, her handmaid and confidant, tiptoed through the door in the king's wake. Sophia turned to her with a playful smile, only to drop it when she saw the deathly pallor of her skin. By the fearful expression etched into Rosemary's lined face, Sophia knew she wasn't going to be lucky. Not at all.

CHAPTER 2

SOPHIA

"**W**HERE DID THIS DRESS come from?" Sophia questioned breathlessly as Rosemary tugged the laces of her bodice tight and tucked them discreetly beneath the fabric. It was a fluffy thing, with bouncing chiffon skirts that would surely make it hard to walk.

"His highness had it made for you when you came of age." Rosemary answered absently, her bottom lip snagged between her teeth as she focused on primping and adjusting the monstrous dress. "Seems you've grown a bit bustier since then."

Sophia glanced down at her scandalously exposed ankles. "And taller."

"Tried to tell his highness you would grow like a beansprout."

Sophia smiled sadly at the older woman's reflection in the mirror. That was Rosemary's nickname for her when she was a gangly young girl, constantly outgrowing her finest gowns. Neither of them had spoken it, not yet willing to admit their grief, but this would be good-bye. Traditionally a princess would take her handmaids with her when she was married off, but Sophia would never ask that of her oldest friend. Rosemary was the closest to a mother Sophia ever had and she wouldn't willingly cause her pain.

Rosemary had a son, David, whose wife was ripe with child. Any day now Rosemary would have a grandchild to cradle and sing lullabies to. David was a shepherd, one of many who suffered losses to his flock since the dragon first darkened their skies. Sophia knew Rosemary was bringing them scraps from the kitchen to fill their bellies while their livelihood suffered. What would happen to their child if Rosemary left to live out the rest of her days in some foreign kingdom?

Sophia had to give her father credit. When he came with news of her "sacrifice" this morning, she hadn't expected to be wed by evening. Clever of him, though she was loath to admit it. Had they offered another feast, celebrating the arrival of a suitor and welcoming him as a guest, Sophia would have had time to scare him away.

Most would say her value was in her beauty and her breeding, but she knew her true talent was making men despise her. Not only men, but any person that dared make her acquaintance. Unfortunately, it wasn't a talent she came by intentionally in the beginning. As a girl Sophia was a lonely, awkward creature, never having the chance to socialize with other girls in the high court.

For reasons she hadn't come to understand, they hated her. She was excluded from every game, unless Rosemary forced them to include her. Even then, they would only see her worthy of playing the queen's handmaid or the blind beggar the queen took pity on. Once they made her crawl around on all fours as the queen's horse, each of them taking turns mounting her and kicking her haunches until they were black and blue.

Perhaps it was for the best that she wouldn't be queen of Calos, despite being the eldest and more experienced. What kind of queen could rule a people that reviled her very existence? That was why Father kept her tucked away since she'd come of age. It was the only kindness the bitter king ever offered her. Sophia would be quietly wed to a lord of some foreign king that offered trade and thus protected her from bloodthirsty subjects that thought her spoiled and unworthy.

A frustrated mewling sound welled from Rosemary's chest, drawing Sophia's attention back to the mirror. The old woman stood behind her, a silky scarlet sash draped across her arm. It was customary for a bride to wear white, signifying purity and promising her maidenhood. Sophia had never seen a bride adorned with any red besides the paint that colored her lips, though the fabric tickled some distant memory in the back of her mind.

Rosemary gripped the sash until her knuckles whitened, murmuring, "There are whispers of a rebellion in your name."

"What?" Sophia pivoted, her lengthy gown tangling around her legs. "A rebellion?"

"The people are scared. That does not mean they condone this sacrifice."

"Rosemary, don't speak another word. It's treason against the king to even ponder such actions." She gripped Rosemary's forearms and met her steely gaze. Rosemary's brown eyes reflected white filigree and painted pale skin back at Sophia.

"I can't let him do this to you, child. I can't stand for it." Rosemary dropped the sash and collapsed into Sophia's arms, wailing and trembling.

"Shhh, don't cry, sweet friend. I'll be alright. Marrying a barbarian king isn't the worst that could happen to me. Perhaps he and I will even learn to enjoy each other's company." She soothed Rosemary's back with her open calm.

Rosemary jerked upright, studying Sophia's face. "Is that what he told you? That you're to be wed?"

Sophia's body became unnaturally still as ice crystallized the blood in her veins. "Is this not a wedding gown? What purpose is there to dress me for a wedding if I'm not to be..." Her sentence died on her tongue as the sash caught the rising afternoon sun, glowing a gory red and mocking her stupidity.

Sacrifice. Her father's choice of words echoed through her mind, each rebound of the sickening phrase melting her frozen state and making her boil with rage. *"You're to make a sacrifice."* The king was not using hyperbole when he chose that particular phrase. Sophia would make a sacrifice. A glittering white and red sacrifice, meant to draw the attention of one fire-breathing, sheep-stealing dragon.

Her morning meal threatened to make a return journey north through her esophagus. Sophia clamped a hand over her mouth and inhaled slowly. When she was sure she wasn't going to hurl all over Rosemary, she removed her fingers and screamed, "Idiot! Wrinkled, useless idiot!"

Rosemary jumped back at the earsplitting noise. "Shush, my lady. You'll alert the guards that wait down the hall." Hands trembling, Rosemary reached for Sophia again. "I can help you. Please, we can steal away from the castle and find the party that would stand for you. They whisper your name, my lady. They speak reverently of *Queen Sophia.*"

Sophia watched tears dry on Rosemary's weathered face. She was a kind woman, kinder than Sophia deserved. And gullible, so very gullible. If men titled her queen, it was only in mockery. If people stood against the king's choice, it was only because they were Gods fearing, devout people and knew the Gods forbade blood sacrifice.

"I cannot let them do this." Rosemary was growing frantic, her eyes flitting between Sophia and the window. "It's only a tale we tell children, the stories of dragon brides. No one knows how your grandsire slayed the dragon. What if it doesn't work? What if the beast takes you and devours you like a lamb, only to return for second helpings? It's wrong. Can't he see it's wrong? His own daughter? *His own daughter?*"

Both women froze at the sound of the chamber door opening. Two king's guard stepped inside, the clinking of their sword belts reminding her of wedding bells.

Rosemary's spine stiffened and she waved angrily at the men. "Get out, the both of you! The princess is not decent. You cannot enter a maiden's chamber without announcing yourself. Now, get!"

Sophia was taken aback by soft-spoken Rosemary's sudden gall. The guards were too, apparently, because they stammered before the taller one hardened his expression and waved two fingers out into the hall. Two young women scurried inside, eyes downcast and cheeks blanched.

"The king wants the princess ready before evening. You're taking too long." The taller guard eyed Rosemary suspiciously. Sophia instinctively stepped in front of her.

"It's my fault." She tittered stupidly and flicked her dark curls over her exposed shoulder. "I'm none too eager to be eaten by a dragon, you understand."

The shorter of the guards visibly winced and the other found somewhere else for his gaze to linger. They mumbled some command that loosely translated to, "hurry up," and left to station themselves outside the door. The two young women bowed their heads apologetically and took up Rosemary's abandoned task. One carefully wrapped the sash around Sophia's waist and began tying a dainty bow in the back while the other vigorously painted Sophia's already colored cheeks with more rouge.

Rosemary could do nothing but gawk helplessly, silent tears wetting the trails of salt left by the previous outburst.

"Don't cry, Rosemary." Sophia spoke to her reflection in the mirror. "I'll be fine."

"But my lady—"

Sophia shushed her with a dark look. "Everything is going to be just fine."

The lie tasted bittersweet. It would keep Rosemary from making an imprudent decision, but Sophia didn't believe it for a second. Deep in her belly fear coiled like a snake preparing to strike.

Or perhaps like a dragon.

CHAPTER 3

SOPHIA

T HE RHYTHMIC TAP OF boots on stone punctuated the short stretches of silence as the king's guard escorted Sophia through the main hall and toward the courtyard. Outside the muffled clang of bells began, sounding haunting rather than celebratory. Today their chimes were a death knell. Sophia simply hadn't died yet. Sweat matted her perfectly curled hair to the back of her neck and trickled between her shoulder blades.

She knew her father saw her as a disappointment, a burden to be discarded on whatever willing suitor he could find, but she thought surely he cared for her enough not to sacrifice her life.

"Sophia" The king's voice startled her out of her angry reverie. He was hovering in the shadows by the doorway, dressed the part in his fine clothing and jeweled crown, not looking particularly kingly with his hunched shoulders and guilty moue.

"Your highness," Sophia kept her gaze focused on the sunlit courtyard, chin raised proud and defiant. Her pride was only to mask the surprising sting of betrayal that was a growing knot in her heart.

Am I truly so worthless alive? Merely a sheep to be slaughtered for divine favor and wealth? That was what she felt like, a sacrifice of old. An innocent life given to appease unforgiving Gods.

"It's the only way."

"Oh? Can you be certain of that? Have you ever dealt with a dragon before?" She tried to hide the devouring fear that was quickly growing into a gaping chasm inside of her, but her voice faltered on the word "dragon."

The king opened beseeching palms. "The people are afraid. I've heard whispers of descent. We must do whatever is necessary to protect your brother's crown."

My brother's crown. Sophia digested the thought with so much bitterness she thought it might make her ill.

"Of course. Gods forbid George has to prove himself to his people the way his namesake did."

"No one knows how Saint George tamed the dragon!" Father hissed.

"Then what is the point of this sacrifice? You're giving your own daughter to a *dragon* based on little more than old wives tales!"

For a fraction of a heartbeat Sophia thought she saw regret tint his eyes. It vanished as quickly as it appeared, leaving a stern and loveless expression in its place. "I was already an old man when I wed your mother. My time as king is coming to an end and I cannot hand the crown to your brother while there is so much unrest."

"Will you shut up and get this over with if I absolve you of your guilt then, old man?" One guard gasped at her harsh remark, but Sophia was fairly certain the other covered a snicker with a loud cough. At least someone found her amusing.

She didn't wait for the king's response or the guards that escorted her. Clinging to whatever pride and bravery she had left, Sophia marched through the castle doorway and into the courtyard. The men and women of the high court were waiting for her, their opulent clothing shimmering in the midday sun. It should have looked cheery and bright, but the colorful fabrics made the courtyard into a macabre painting, teeming with foreboding whispers.

Some of the ladies appeared pale and one or two men offered remorseful nods. The energy in the crowd was otherwise excited. Of course, it was. The high court wasn't made up of lords and ladies but bloodthirsty animals with twisted appetites. Or maybe those man-eating fish with teeth that Sophia once read about.

A hysterical giggle erupted from her throat at the mental image of flopping, toothy fish wearing colorful gowns and tunics.

Eyes widened and the whispers turned to a horrified buzz at the sound of her laughter. Right, because she was the unhinged one. Nothing crazy about sacrificing a princess to a dragon to make it go away.

"Come along then, you well dressed baboons!" Sophia sang over her shoulder, her steps jaunty as she made her way outside the castle walls and into the city streets. If she was going to die, she might as well enjoy herself. Armor clattered as her guards raced to catch up to her, gently gripping her forearms to prevent her from fleeing.

The procession of the high court, surrounded by king's guard and led by Sophia, quickly drew a crowd. The streets swelled with people, their voices hushed and their faces somber. For some reason Sophia had expected worse of them. Perhaps jeering and whoops of joy at the thought of the spoiled princess meeting her doom in the maw of a dragon. At the very least she thought they'd be pleased at the prospect of the dragon leaving their flocks alone and no longer sending them ducking for cover in the middle of the day.

No one jeered. In fact, twice Sophia caught the eye of women standing in the streets and saw them visibly weeping. Were they afraid of the gore that might follow? Or perhaps that the dragon would gain

a taste for maidens when he was finished picking his teeth of her and
come back for seconds?

Sweat beaded her brow as they passed the stone temple, the last
building in the city before the outer gate. Glass depictions of angels
and the great Saint George himself glittered beautifully. The very last
decorative window drew her attention, the red of flames appearing too
realistic in the sunlight. The fire came as a stream, pouring from the
lips of a great gold dragon. A dry lump formed in her throat, and she
swallowed painfully.

Sophia was marching herself—rather proudly—to her death. What
was she thinking? What did she care if she showed a brave face in front
of the people of Calos? The people who *hated* her? The sacrificial
procession came to a lurching halt when Sophia stopped just before
the outer gate. She dug her heels into the gravelly road, sending puffs
of dust up to dirty the hem of her pristine white dress.

Panic clawed at her like a wild animal and she mimicked it, writhing
in the grip of the two guards. A low keening noise escaped her throat
and she kicked at the guard to her right. Sophia wasn't a particularly
petite woman but her meager strength was no match for two trained
soldiers. Their meaty hands tightened on her arms and with a grunt,
they propelled her forward out of the city gates and toward the rolling
green hills.

"No!" Sophia wailed. "I won't be your sacrifice!"

A low murmur rippled through the crowd. The king's guard closed
ranks around the people of the high court and their pace quickened
until Sophia's feet were practically dragging on the ground. The lower
half of her dress was becoming a filthy brown color and the red sash
billowed behind her like a flag.

Her heart sank as they crested a hill, stopping before the great
stone pillar. The base of the stone was stained by half a century of

blood. Once the Gods were much hungrier, more demanding of their children. Was this dragon a new form of divinity? A God come down from the heavens to take the skin of a beast and torment the people who were not devout enough?

Or perhaps the myth about dragons and maidens was true and Sophia was to be the bride of some foul creature.

Another manic laugh choked her. How very clever of her father. This was one suitor she couldn't scare away with her prickly manner.

"Sophia, dearest sister." A voice cut through the dull buzz that filled her skull.

Sophia had gone completely numb, losing track of time and her surroundings as defeat swallowed her whole. She looked down to find a thick rope binding her hands together, tethering her to a heavy wooden stake.

"Sophia," Warm hands cupped her cheeks, smearing the tears she hadn't realized she was shedding. Sympathetic blue eyes blinked at her. "Be at peace, sister. This is not your end."

Her brother's words were meant to be kind. Instead, they felt like the cruelest betrayal of all. Were they not on the same side? Wasn't it his duty to stand against injustice? A new anger burned away her numbness. "A dragon is going to eat me. How can I be at peace?"

"You're not to be a meal. You're to be a bride."

"Oh, a *bride*? Will the dragon be joining us for a feast? Do you think he'll fit inside the dining hall? Or in my bed, for that matter? How am I to fulfill my wifely duty with a monster whose cock is bigger than you?" George wasn't the only one to gasp at her unladylike outburst. She remembered absently that it was not only her father, her brother, and the blabbering priest saying some prayer standing atop the hillside, but most of the population of Calos.

Despite her acrimonious reaction, her brother maintained a calm demeanor. "Please, trust me, Sophia. Don't fight when the beast takes you."

"Don't fight? *Don't fight?*" She'd had enough of stupid men stupidly telling her what to do. They could hate her all they wanted, but that didn't mean she deserved death by dragon. "I hope you get pox on your genitals! I hope your firstborn son has the head of a goat! I hope your future queen runs away with a hairy barbarian king!"

A roar of laughter rolled through the crowd. *That* cracked George's mask of regal calm. His face turned a familiar shade of red, making a striking impression of their father. Her face was likely a similar color after his palm connected with her cheek.

"If you'd done your duty and married any of the many lords we uselessly paraded around the castle, you wouldn't be in this mess. *You* acted the part of the shrew, Sophia. You can only blame yourself."

"No, I can blame whoever bound my hands and wrapped me up like a juicy turkey. It is definitely their fault." Sophia turned away from her brother, her heart aching as much as her cheek. Her gaze landed on a young man standing behind the closest king's guard. His eyes burned with furious intensity, and he nodded solemnly at Sophia.

She watched with growing curiosity as he reached into his pocket, retrieving a handkerchief of bright red and tying it tightly around his upper arm. Another man to his left did the same, followed by another and another.

"Long live Queen Sophia!" The first man called, raising his red-banded arm in the air.

"Long live Queen Sophia!" A chorus of deep voices repeated the cry. Sophia's gaze roamed the crowd, noting dozens more people wearing red handkerchiefs. Her eyes faltered on Rosemary, the red contrasting brightly against her grey smock.

*They're standing with me? **For** me?*

"What is the meaning of this?" The king bawled so loudly that his crown slipped down onto his forehead. He straightened the sparkling gold headpiece and glowered at the shouting men and women. "This is treasonous speak! Need I remind you what the punishment for treason is?"

A hush quickly fell over the crowd. He didn't need to remind them; the remains of previously punished rebels were scattered about their feet, bones half buried in the soil, ground to dust by time. The history of Calos was a bloody one and the current king was only a generation removed from tyranny.

The first young man ignored the king's warning, shouting, "The people will not stand behind a cowardly king! We will not stand for sacrifice!"

A guard turned and violently yanked the young man's arm, tossing him to the ground. A leather boot raised, ready to smash the poor man's face when an unusual cloud zipped across the hills to shadow them. As one, the crowd raised their eyes to the sky. Seconds later a great wind buffeted colorful gowns and carefully braided hair. A woman shrieked; a man shouted some incoherent curse. Both were answered with a vicious, deafening roar.

Then chaos reigned down on the people of Calos in streams of scorching fire.

CHAPTER 4

SOPHIA

THE LATE SUMMER AFTERNOON was already sweltering when the dragon arrived. Now, Sophia wasn't entirely sure she hadn't been lit on fire. Flames crackled violently around her, close enough that she seemed to be melting. Sweat soaked her tarnished gown and her skin was so slick she could almost slip her hands free of the ropes binding her wrist.

Almost.

Screams bounced around the hillside, coming from every direction. People stumbled through the grassy fields toward the safety of the outer walls, shoving each other and clustering together like frightened sheep. More than one person was trampled. Minutes ago, Sophia would have prayed they found their death beneath thundering feet. That was before they raised their voices in rebellious support.

Long live Queen Sophia.

Unfortunately, she wouldn't live long enough to become a queen of anything, except maybe bones. Flames licked at her back, making her skin prickle painfully. She yelped and tugged helplessly at the wooden stake. It wouldn't matter if she freed herself. There was a dragon—Gods have mercy, *a dragon*—flapping enormous, leathery wings above her.

His scales were the color of gilded dusk. Molten reptilian eyes bore down on her. Sophia saw her reflection in them and froze. They were sparkling treasure and a promise of death all at once.

How could a creature be so horrible and beautiful?

"Not beautiful, just horrible! *Horrible!*" She shrieked when a clawed hand swooped low to the ground, wrapping tightly around her waist and lifting her, wooden stake and all, off the hillside.

The dragon was by far the biggest beast she'd ever seen, but not quite as big as he looked from the safety of the castle. His scaly, clawed hand was only large enough to circle her ribs, making her feel like an errant child being carried away by her mother. One fabric shoe slipped from her helplessly dangling foot and Sophia shrieked again when she saw just how far the shoe fell before it hit the ground. They were rising into the sky. Rapidly.

In some other circumstance, the view might have been lovely. The lush hills of Calos, perfect for grazing livestock, were like green waves. They washed to the walls of the kingdom, a shore made of grey stone and dark wood. Tiny dots of color, the people who had only moments ago been circling her, melded together as they trickled through the gate.

That was all Sophia could see before the wind picked up tenfold, whipping strands of hair across her eyes. Her gown billowed up around her, exposing her legs and torso to the chilled air. It was so cold that the prickles rising on her skin were painful. In contrast to the biting wind, the dragon's scales were hot to the touch, almost uncomfortably so. Heat leeched into her torso, only to be gusted away.

At least he hasn't eaten me. The hopeful thought lasted mere breaths before her mind conjured an image of a graveyard carpeted with the bones of maidens, the dragon's private dining hall.

Sophia clung to the claws that were nearly puncturing her skin for an eternity before she felt brave enough to brush hair from her eyes. She got a brief glimpse of rocky outcroppings and steeply sloped hills dotted with porous volcanic stone.

Just when Sophia thought she was going to freeze to death, they began to descend. Suddenly the wind was coming from one direction, blowing straight into her face and removing the obstruction of her hair so she could see jagged rocks jetting up from the sides of the mountain. They appeared to be coming at her far too fast. No way could this creature land on three legs at that speed.

Forget being burned alive, Sophia was going to die by impalement.

She screamed until her throat was raw, weather sharpened stone pointing straight at her. At the last moment the dragon banked to the right, tucking its wings, and dropping them into a narrow opening that seemed far too small for such a creature. The hidden tunnel was deceptive, its dark entrance looming over the rest and hiding the vast cave that carved into the mountain side.

Sophia expected darkness. Instead beams of silvery light filled the natural corridor, catching on the exposed surface of crystals and precious gems, creating a lovely sparkling effect.

The tunnel widened and Sophia gasped at the massive space. They appeared to be inside a great hall, with rough stone pillars holding up the high ceiling. More crystals lined the walls. Firelight coming from unknown sources turned them a glittering shade of gold.

She couldn't tell if this was a natural cave system or if it had been carved by the long dead mountain dwellers, a forgotten home of the ancestors of Calos. It made sense that the dragon would make this place his nest. Legend said the ancient people discovered dragons deep under the mountains while they mined for precious gems and gold. It was because of them that the monsters darkened the sky, terrorizing the people who first settled the valley.

Sophia grunted when the clawed hand released her, setting her too hard on her feet and sending a sharp pain through her ankles. She stood frozen in terror, waiting for the bath of fire that would roast her like a pig on the spit. The heat was much milder than she expected, almost pleasant. Slowly, feigning bravery, Sophia pivoted to look at her abductor. It was the dragon's breath that warmed her back and not the kind that toasted sheep. The creature was eyeing her with yellow-gold eyes, a thin black slit of pupil shifting with the flickering fire light.

His scaly snout was mere inches from her. Any moment the dragon could open his mouth and swallow her whole, if she was lucky. If not, he might chew her up slowly with those massive teeth. In the dim light of the cave, he could almost blend into the walls. His own mass shadowed his sunset belly, making him look like a stone with bright cat eyes.

"Well?" Sophia prodded, ready to get this over with. She didn't know if she could take another moment of fear.

Fear was overtaken by anger when the dragon continued studying her. The rage and indignation at her father's actions, at the sudden revelation that perhaps she wasn't hidden away because she was hated but rather because she was dangerous to her brother's rule, erupted from her in a rush of foolish bravado. Her leg was extending, connecting with the dragon's jaw before she could think better of it.

"You stupid reptile! Stupid, stupid lizard!" One kick turned into a flurry of them. She was spitting mad, cursing the beast. "If you're not going to eat me then take me back! Take me back right now." She scowled at the monster, trying to cross her arms only to realize her hands were still bound to a long wooden stake. "I don't know if you noticed, but I was in the middle of a very important rebellion when you so rudely interrupted."

The dragon jerked his head in surprise, letting out a chuffing sound that she wanted to call amusement. The amusement gave way to a rumble of warning and the show of teeth when she kicked him again. There was that fear once more, chilling her to the core and making her heart beat so rapidly she thought it might overwork itself and fail.

The creature took on a strange glow, his shape contorting. He seemed to be writhing and... Shrinking? Smaller and smaller the dragon grew until his claws retracted, the strange horns that adorned his head receded, and the scales smoothed out into taut bronze flesh. That fearsome snout flattened into a very human face.

And suddenly, where once stood a dragon was now a man. Naked, muscled man with skin the color of that golden dragon underbelly. The only detail that hadn't changed, the only indication that Sophia hadn't lost her mind in a fit of fear, was those gilded eyes. The slit pupils opened up into wells of black, widened in shock and horror.

Why in the world was he shocked and horrified? Sophia just watched him transform from a dragon.

"Eat you? Why would I eat you?" His timbre bounced across the cave walls and came crashing into her the way that hot dragon breath had. Sophia shuddered at the unexpectedly rich sound, feeling as if his voice somehow matched the beautiful gold color of him.

She stood there for as many heartbeats as it took for her to tongue to become unstuck from the roof of her mouth. Then she stupidly muttered, "You're not a dragon," before falling into a dizzy heap on the floor.

CHAPTER 5

BURNE

S HE FAINTED. CLOSE ENOUGH, anyway. The woman was curled on the ground, her hands covering her face and her body looking too limp for a conscious person. She was brave enough to kick a dragon—she *kicked* him—but couldn't face a naked man.

He was in good form last he checked, but certainly not fetching enough to make a woman woozy. Really, he expected much more from a witch. Weren't they known for their wicked deeds? She acted more modest and flustered than a maiden on her wedding night.

He cleared his throat and cautiously crouched beside her. "Are you alright?"

Frizzy, dark curls curtained her face. Her unkempt hair was surprising considering that she was robed in a luxurious wedding gown. Or it had been luxurious before smoke and dust left patches of discoloration all over the bright white fabric. A bodice of lace filigree climbed her torso to rest beneath her collarbones.

His attention caught on the most alluring piece of the ensemble. A red sash was tied around her slender waist, accentuating the round of her hips and drawing the gaze to her bosom—if it were not hidden by her trembling arms. Without his dragon sight, it was an ordinary color. It contrasted with the gown dramatically, the only color in this part of the cave save for the orange hues of firelight, but it was not such a flag for his attention in this state.

When he took his dragon form, he sacrificed some advantages to gain others. Momentarily losing his ability to see color seemed a small price to pay for wings and a maw that could capture a warhorse. The exception, he'd found, was the color red. For some reason it was as bright and brilliant in both forms. And another oddity? His dragon loved the sight of it. Until this day he'd thought it morbid, a fascination with the macabre scene left when he finished feasting.

Then he saw her. The witch. Wind whipped the sash behind her, a seductive dance of red to draw him in. As he neared, he noticed not only the fabric but the rosy tinge to her cheeks, her pomegranate lips. He could only imagine what other parts of her were a blushing shade of red.

"Am I alright?" She dragged her palms down her face, parting her hair to gawk at him.

Her eyes were bloodshot and unfocused—probably a side effect of flying. She would have been beautiful if the expression on her face wasn't quite so *murderous*. Azure eyes churned with fury, her thin nose wrinkled to match the snarl of those plush lips. Her jaw was prominent enough for her chin to jut out stubbornly.

"Am I *alright*?" She repeated. "No, you stupid lizard man!" A delicate hand swatted at him, narrowly missing his bare chest as he jerked back. "I am most certainly not *alright!*"

She remembered he could turn into a fire breathing beast, right?

With a petulant pout, she crossed her arms over her bust and flopped back onto her bottom. The fabric of her gown tangled her legs and she wrestled with it for more than a minute before it was tame enough to lie flat.

"Stupid dress! Stupid king! Stupid lizard!"

"*Lizard?* A dragon is not a lizard," he argued, feeling insulted.

"That's precisely what a dragon is. A big, flying lizard. You're a reptile." Somehow, she managed to make that one word become the most scathing title he'd ever received.

"You're being surprisingly ungrateful considering that I rescued you."

She laughed bitterly. "Rescued me? From what exactly?"

"From being burned." He mirrored her crossed arms and sat back on his heels.

"You rescued me? From being burned?" Her words dripped with sardonic sweetness. "You nearly burned me alive!"

He resisted pointing out that his fire couldn't hurt her seeing as she was *his*. She was not as amicable as he'd anticipated, and he suspected divulging that information wouldn't bode well for this already sour conversation. "I had no intention of burning you, or anyone else if it could be avoided. I was merely scaring away that blood hungry flock. I couldn't very well let them execute you."

She stared blankly at him. "You thought they were going to execute me?"

Why wouldn't he think that? The last time he was awake in Calos, that hilltop had been used for all manner of killing. Most often sharp tongued women and disobedient wives were burned for "witchcraft."

"For being a witch."

Her laughter was real this time, honey sweet and pleasant, though far too boisterous to be the delicate response of a lady. It warmed him all the way to his bones, causing him to smile like a dopey boy. He was never going to hear enough of that sound.

"No one has been burned for being a witch in Calos for almost half a century." One hand clutched her belly, more laughter tumbling out. "They were trying to sacrifice me to *the dragon*. It appears they were at least half successful." Her eyes flicked briefly over his body. Though her expression was bold, her cheeks pinked and she didn't let her gaze fall below his navel. "What is your name, dragon man?"

He had so many more questions for her, but he held them back. She was calming, her scent of summer flowers no longer heavy with the cloying taste of her fear.

"Burne,"

"Burn?" She blinked. "You're a dragon, named *Burn*?" More laughter ensued. "Very funny indeed, lizard fellow."

"A *dragon* is not a *lizard*." His jaw tensed. "Burne was my grandfather's name. I was called that to honor him. It's spelled with an 'E,' though I suppose I do see the humor in it now." He cracked a smile, trying not to let her mockery put him in a mood. The day had been harrowing for her. "What is yours?"

"Sophia." She answered primly. "I am princess Sophia Saint George, rightful heir to the throne of Calos."

Burne's heart dislodged from its resting place in his breast and sank down to his toes. Sophia *Saint George*? His bride, whose delicious scent carried on the wind to call him away from his hunt, was the daughter of his sworn enemy.

CHAPTER 6

BURNE

"KING GEORGE IS YOUR father?" Burne scrubbed a palm down his face. He wouldn't call that bastard a Saint.

"King Bancroft is my father. Saint George was my grandfather." She cocked her head, eyebrows arching in a way that looked mocking and dignified at once. "Why does that make you look ill? Are you afraid I'll slay you?"

"Afraid of a slight woman in a bridal gown? Ridiculous." *Liar. You shouldn't lie to her.* Burne stood abruptly and turned away from her, not wanting to reveal any more in his expression. Reticence was never his strong suit.

Sophia cleared her throat loudly. "Well, now that we've got this misunderstanding sorted, perhaps you could take me back? I was experiencing a rather exciting revelation before you kidnapped me. Oh, and I would appreciate it if you could stop terrorizing my people while you're at it. Surely there is plenty for you to eat in the forests and fields beyond Calos."

"No." One word, clipped so she didn't hear the growl rising in his chest. It wouldn't do to frighten her again, not if he intended for her to stay.

Did he still want her to stay now that he'd discovered her pedigree? Yes. He couldn't help it, would never be able to live with great distances between them now. It was the curse of his kind, or perhaps the failsafe designed by whatever deity created them. Once the dragon chose a mate, they would never want for another. He would live and die for her, whether he liked her or not.

Only sons were born as *Drakonmein*. There were no females of their kind, not a single woman born with the strength of a Demi-god and the magic to shift to the form of a dragon. That meant any and all dragon mates were human women, vulnerable and fragile, so easily stolen away.

So easy to use as leverage.

Burne balled his fists, only barely resisting the urge to pummel the nearest pillar. It would only serve to frighten her, and if he was even more unlucky, bring down half the ceiling.

"No?" The rustling of silky fabric told him that Sophia had risen from her place on the floor. "You intend to keep me prisoner? Or perhaps you're going to eat me after all?"

Burne turned on her with a predatory smile, crowding her until she backed into a stone pillar. "You keep suggesting I might eat you. I'm beginning to think that you want me to, princess."

"And I'm beginning to think you have all the intelligence of a skink." There was that proud chin again. She was not easily cowed, he had to give her that.

Burne felt a small surge of pride despite himself. Strength of character was a very desirable trait in a mate.

A mate whose grandsire was responsible for destroying his family.

"I will not keep you prisoner." He considered, knowing he couldn't keep her here unwilling. He also knew he wouldn't be satisfied until he understood her loyalties and desires. "I only ask for your company, for a time."

"My company? Ah, even a dragon man is not immune to feminine wiles. What kind of company, pray tell? Do you wish for me to dine and dance, flouncing around in this ridiculous dress and smiling coyly? Shall I titter and bat my eyes each time you speak?" She ducked beneath his arms and grabbed her skirts, swishing them this way and that with a flirtatious smile on her lips. "Or perhaps you want a baser sort of company. Do you wish me to remove my gown and bare myself to you? That's the end goal for every man that attends feasts and festivals for my *company*. There is no conquest so sweet as wooing a maiden, am I wrong?"

Burne glared at her, completely befuddled. He wasn't sure if he should laugh at her mockery, be furious at the prospect of other men wooing her, or demand she fulfill her final remark by ripping her gown away. She would be a sweet conquest, indeed.

But she was so much more than that and Burne needed to convince her as much.

Instead of responding, he swept an arm around her waist and jerked her toward him. She gasped, giving his free hand the perfect opportunity to snatch her jaw and pry her mouth open. Sophia squealed and smacked him but it was no use. She couldn't hurt him, not with those delicate, unworked hands.

"What are you doing?" She finally managed to shake her head from his grip.

"I was looking for the barbs on your tongue." Sophia took several stumbling steps back and he had a wild urge to prowl after her. Instead, he said, "give me three days."

"Three days?"

"Have you noticed there is an echo in this cave?"

Sophia glowered at him. She was very good at making that particular expression. Burne hoped that she wasn't too pettish. "What do you wish to do with me during these three days?"

Oh, I have so many wicked wishes, my dear Sophia.

"Teach me what has happened since your grandfather George was king. Tell me of the modern world outside these mountains. Share stories with me, meals with me."

"Do you expect me to share your bed, too?" She swept the main hall with suspicious eyes. "Do you even have a bed?"

"I have many and I will not ask you to join me in mine." *Not until you beg for it on your own accord.* "I've been alone in this mountain for a long time. Half a century, apparently."

Now those suspicious eyes were burning into him. "How old are you? You don't look a day over five and twenty."

"I will answer your questions if you answer mine."

A scheme was forming behind that beautiful face, he could tell. Sophia chewed her bottom lip, her pointer finger absently tapping her chin. When she finally gave a subtle nod and fixated back on him, Burne felt, for the very first time in his life, as if he were prey.

"You want three days with me?"

"Yes."

"And you don't expect me to surrender my maidenhood to you?"

Gods, I pray that you will. "No."

"Very well. I have conditions." Of course, she did. Was he destined to mate a mad woman? She was thousands of feet above the valley, deep in a cave system only accessible by flight or secret tunnel, and she thought she could negotiate. Her boldness was tantalizing.

Burne considered giving her a flat no, just to see if her reaction would be as petulant as he anticipated, but he was too curious—and admittedly a little too eager to please her—to refuse. "What conditions are these?"

"One, you will not go back on your word. I have no intention to climb into your bed. Two, you answer any and all questions I ask." She flicked one finger up into the air, then another. At least she only had ten fingers. "Three, at the end of the third day, you will return me to my home. And four," her eyes flashed in the firelight, looking like sapphires. "You will stop terrorizing Calos."

"One, I am not a barbarian and would find no joy in taking an unwilling woman." Burne stuck out his own finger. "Two, I will answer your questions only if you also answer mine. Three, I will return you to your home on the third day, *if you still wish to go.*" He moved closer to her as he spoke, gravitating towards those smug lips until he could taste her breath. "Four, I am not terrorizing anyone."

"Not terrorizing—what do you call flying over farms, burning fields, and massacring sheep?"

He traced her bottom lip with his thumb. "Breaking my fast."

For a short breath, she was mesmerized by his touch, feeling the heat that sparked between them. If Burne had any doubt about the dragon's choice of mate, that simple touch incinerated it. The pad of his thumb burned with a fire that was all pleasure and no pain. Gods, he wanted to let those flames lap at his bare skin, wanted her to take those petite hands and press them into his chest.

"N-no more," her voice quavered but she managed to finish her thought. "You cannot take from the farmers anymore." She shoved his hand away. "And please remember that this is *not* a seduction."

"What is it then, Sophia?" He purred, enjoying the blush that pinked her cheeks.

"Five," Sophia ignored his question. "Clothe yourself."

"You're not pleased with what you see?"

She turned her back on him. "I don't know what game it is you want to play with me, lizard man, but I will not participate."

"Oh, but Sophia, you've just agreed to do exactly that."

CHAPTER 7

SOPHIA

T HE HEAVY FABRIC OF her gown rustled as Sophia whirled again, taking in the space around her with the same awe as she had the first four times. The dragon's cave was not a cave at all, rather a secret castle, carefully dug into the heart of the mountain. The entrance was nothing of notice and the main hall where she'd made her agreement with Burne was cold and uninviting, despite the firelight. But this? This was like a dream.

They stood in a dining hall. More fire flickered on candelabras artfully crafted from stone, burning some form of magic rather than fuel. Overhead the high ceiling was a rough, natural shape. Sophia found it far more enchanting than the precise architecture and painted depictions of heaven in her father's dining hall. Thousands of precious gems jutted out from the stone in a glittering show. There were so many varying colors that Sophia was sure there were hues she'd never seen before.

Father couldn't afford to *stand beneath* these gems, much less dream of owning them.

Yet it wasn't the luxury that had Sophia enchanted—yes, she was very much enchanted, despite her best efforts to remain untouched by this strange and unexpected place. It was the magic that had her enthralled. *Real* magic. Before today she believed in magic, but she'd never witnessed it with her own eyes.

First there was Burne—Sophia studied him, thankfully clothed, with a furtive gaze—and his *ability*. Now there was this...Gods, she couldn't bring herself to call it a dining hall. To her, it felt a place of worship. Energy hummed in the air, warming a space which ought to have been cold and damp.

It was warming the food, too. Plates and plates of meats, pies, fire-roasted vegetables, and much more lined a dark dining table. The hall was fit to feed twenty people, not two, and the feast was as well. Try as she might, Sophia couldn't fathom where it had come from. Were there servants tucked away in this secret cave? Did they have a tunnel of their own to access the ground, coming and going to markets right under the noses of the people of Calos?

And if he had such feasts at his disposal, why was the dragon thinning flocks of sheep and mowing down herds of cattle?

Sophia voiced the question aloud and received only the vaguest answer.

"It's in my nature."

"Is that how you plan to answer all of my questions? You should know, patience is not in *my* nature." Sophia paced along one side of the table, studying platters of food and putting much needed space between her and Burne.

"I've gathered as much." He walked parallel to her, eyeing her over the table like she was to be served on a platter along with the roast duck. She needed to tread very carefully where he was concerned. "My answers will be more forthcoming when you give me some of your own."

"Hardly seems a fair exchange." She was tempted to pluck some kind of candied cherry from a tray but thought better of it. Magical food was often used to trick and trap young women in the stories from her childhood.

Reading her thoughts, Burne offered, "it won't harm you. Eat your fill."

"I have little reason to trust you."

"I've given you no reason not to trust me." He countered.

"You took the form of a dragon, snatched me up from my home, and hid me away in your impenetrable mountain castle. Now you're holding me captive. I find none of that inspires trust."

"I'm not holding you captive." Somehow Burne moved around the edge of the table at an incredible speed, startling a gasp from her when he appeared right before her with a cherry between finger and thumb. "Try it."

"It's not a trick?"

She noticed for the first time that his eyes were no longer that glowing shade of gold but instead a swirling red jasper with gilded veins. His pupils were wider and more human until her attention jumped to his tongue, which was slowly wetting his lips. That black pools narrowed to fine lines, the gold overtaking red-brown. A strange noise filled the space between them. Sophia was reminded of the heavy purring sound the castle cats made when they were scratched just right.

"Trust me, Sophia." His voice was as rough as the carved stone walls. A shiver tickled down her spine, the words seeming to rumble across her skin.

It was then, when her guard momentarily slipped, that she noticed he was rather handsome. For a dragon man, anyway. A defined jaw framed those distracting lips. His nose was broad and masculine, neither too small nor too big for his face. Those ever changing eyes were strange, very strange, but they were undeniably beautiful too.

Sophia watched his hair in the shifting firelight, wondering at the texture of it. Would it be soft if she were to run her fingers through it? It was unlike any hair she'd seen before. Silken locks hung just below the corners of his jaw. The way the light played on it, she almost believed his hair to be made up of thousands of gilded threads. It truly looked like gold.

Burne's mouth kicked up in a smoldering smile, his fingers pressing her lips open to gently feed her the sweet. The cherry was the perfect ripeness—impossible since the season for them hadn't quite begun—and the sugary coating was just the right amount of sweet to counter the fruit's tartness.

A noise rolled off her tongue that was disturbingly close to a moan. Sophia quickly ducked her gaze and went back to studying the table.

"Who made all of this? Do you have servants here?" She picked up some kind of roll and sniffed it.

"It's a spell." Burne explained, making a similar sound to her as he tongued a cherry. "Gods, I have missed these."

"A spell? Is this food real? Will it sate our hunger?"

"Yes. It is a glutton's spell. You can sate your hunger endlessly. This particular magic was a mating gift, given to my great grandmother by a powerful witch. Whenever there is a mistress in this hall, a glorious feast will appear, featuring the foods that will please her most." He took a seat before an empty plate and gestured for her to do the same beside him.

Sophia perched on the very edge of the bench, as far from him as she could manage. The plates and cutlery were only set for two and the placement was intimate enough that their elbows touched. She would have moved herself but the table was so laden that there wasn't space.

Sophia continued studying the food, noting that quite a few of the featured dishes were her favorites. "And where is this mistress of yours? Does she know I'm here?"

"You're quite familiar with her."

"You infuriating man—lizard!" Sophia picked up her fork and stabbed a piece of glazed pork, stuffing it in her mouth with little regard for table manners. It was her favorite preparation of pork. She dropped her fork and instead took the next bite between her fingers, licking the sticky sauce from them loudly. Father would be horrified.

Burne was very far from horrified. His pupils shrank again. Sophia wasn't sure if it was frightening or thrilling. Perhaps both.

"Why are you looking at me that way? I am not a platter of meat to be devoured. And I won't be good company if you refuse to answer my questions plainly." She reached for another dish, gripping the leg of a pheasant and biting it in the most barbaric way. Another bite and she couldn't hold back her pleasured groan. "Gods, this is incredible. I love pheasant seasoned this way. It's truly magic? It will appear again? An endless supply? I could fatten up more than a summer hog."

Burne didn't answer. His amused attention was still fixated on her unladylike show of appetite. She sampled a fourth meal, sweet carrots cooked just so, and felt a sudden loss of hunger as her stomach soured. They were her *favorite* carrots. Her favorite pork, her favorite pheasant, her favorite cherries—even the herbed roll she'd been sniffing was one she enjoyed.

"I will not be your mistress, by any definition of the word. Just because my father saw fit to sacrifice me to you does not mean I will surrender."

"You have a lot to say, princess."

"Queen." She corrected primly. "My people want me as queen." And it was only making her a *little* full in the head.

"You were to be a sacrifice to *me*? They still do that?"

"Still? I thought the only other attempt was princess Ruby, rescued by my great grandfather before the dragon could take her." Burne was incredibly talented in the art of distraction. Each of his musings was vague enough to nip at her curiosity and cause her to forget her ire—the armor that protected her from men like him.

Not men quite like him. I have never been courted by a dragon man before. Not that this was a courting. No felicitous marriage ever began with kidnapping.

"There have been many dragons and many maidens given to them. Your kind would call it sacrifice. My kind call it a marriage. Not all marriages are born of love, not initially. Do they not keep history in your kingdom anymore?" He took a thoughtful bite of pork. "Perhaps not. Otherwise you would know the real story of King George."

"I've had enough of these word games. Speak plainly to me. How old are you? What are these sacrifices you claim to know if? And why do you hold such hostility against Saint George? Is it merely because he slayed the dragon, another like you?"

"Oh, but there is so much to cover and I am so enjoying this conversation."

Sophia chose to take a different approach this time and remain silent, focusing on her food and enjoying every bite.

Burne watched her until she'd eaten more than was comfortable before speaking again. "There are many myths about my kind and our origin. No one knows where the *Drakonmein* came from, including the *Drakonmein*. I am the last living generation of the dragons of Calos, perhaps the last living dragon anywhere. I know of others like me but I have not spoken to them in many, many years. Some believe the dragons were placed here by the Gods to look after the realms. Others believe they were meant to rule them. I am of the opinion that a good ruler protects his realm above his own interests.

"That is a lesson my father taught me. According to him, we were kings once. By day, my grandfather sat upon the throne of Calos. By night, he took to the skies on the wings of a dragon, guarding over all the land and people that were his. His queen was not a highborn lady, but a washer woman's daughter. She was what your people now call a sacrifice. She was one of many offered on the same hill where I found you, but she was the only one the dragon chose.

"You see, Sophia, my kind are not like men. They do not hunger for just any young flesh they can get their hands on. They do not pursue one woman out of lust and another out of duty. We are beholden to the creature we become. It is he who chooses the bride for us and he will allow no other once he has chosen. A dragon's mate is forever. It is a bond stronger than marriage, that extends beyond death. *Drakonmein* will die for a mate. And sometimes, they die without one.

"It is our greatest flaw and it is how your grandfather came to be a king. He learned this secret and used it against my grandfather to take his throne. George was a knight, not particularly strong, but clever. He stole away with the queen, holding her captive and threatening her life until the dragon came. She was his vulnerability and George exploited it. My grandsire had no choice but to surrender himself for his queen. That too is in our nature.

"You, *Queen Sophia*," his voice dripped with sarcasm, "are the daughter of a usurper, a liar, and a murderer."

Sophia shoved her plate away and stood from the table so quickly her head spun. "A liar? You make accusations so easily against others when it's you who is lying. How dare you! Why spin such a tale? Is it my throne you're after?"

"I speak only the truth. It has been covered up and forgotten by your family. As for the why? I don't know. There are too many whys that I have no answer to. Why did Lady Fate give me you, of all people?" She couldn't tell if he was angry, sad, or amused. There was such emotion tied to the story he told that Sophia didn't doubt he believed it. Burne was not lying, he was simply mad.

Of course, he was. He wasn't an ordinary man. He was half beast and beasts were nothing but blood thirsty, rut-hungry monsters.

"I will not sit here and listen to this slander. There are a great many things I cannot explain about you or this place, but that doesn't mean I will blindly trust your twisted explanation. Goodnight, lizard."

Even before Sophia learned to speak, her maids claimed she had a hot temper. She would stamp her feet and squeal over the silliest struggles, ripping apart a dress because the frills were itchy or tossing food at her brother because his squalling was too loud for her to be heard. The longer she was with Burne, the more she felt like that angry child again.

Her bare feet—she'd lost her shoes in flight—slapped against stone as she stormed out of the dining room and into a narrow hall. Sophia hadn't the faintest clue where it led. She knew only that she needed to get away from that insufferable man—lizard!

The tunnel was darker than the hall, featuring only dim candles every ten feet. She passed several locked doors, yanking the handle on each with no success, until she ducked out of the poor light and into an open room.

Two lonely candles burned on a desk across from the doorway. Other than the thin beam of light that came through the crack in the door when she opened it, Sophia couldn't see anything to identify what kind of room it was. It would suit her sulking requirements so long as it wasn't a dungeon.

She closed the door behind her and hurried to the desk, suddenly feeling anxious being alone in such an ill-lit place. There was no telling what Burne might keep in his underground kingdom. Goblins and ogres could be waiting in the shadows. After consuming a feast served entirely by magic, who was she to say they weren't real?

When she reached the desk, Sophia found unlit candles balanced in candelabras scattered on every open surface. A shelf filled with decorative pieces of crystal, a chest of drawers, a boudoir table—endless pieces of lavish furniture. She rushed through the room as fast as she dared, lighting every candle in sight. Eventually she recognized a luxurious fireplace highlighted by some kind of glossy, black stone.

Logs waited in the hearth, dry and perfect for the roaring fire she craved. It was cold being in the heart of a mountain and her ruined gown did little to keep the heat from evaporating off her skin. Flames devoured the kindling she fed to the tip of a lit candle. It wasn't long before the fireplace blazed with life, giving her an excellent view of the other half of the room.

A massive canopy bed hovered in the shadowed half of the chamber. Its curtains were pulled open, it's velvety blankets and plush pillows arranged neatly. At that moment Sophia became aware of just how tired she was. Morning seemed a hundred years ago and her body ached from tension.

If she was to stay here for days, she would need to sleep. Surely Burne understood that. This room had little personal accent, nothing to make it feel like a home. Sophia thought it safe to assume it was a guest room.

Of all the luxuries Burne's castle housed, this bed was by far the greatest. Even better than the magic food. Another spell had to be at work, otherwise how was it possible for any surface to be that soft? The very essence of her being was cocooned into the mattress.

If only she could get comfortable enough to sleep. Sophia lay stiffly atop the blanket, not wanting to climb under and soil the sheets with her filthy gown. The air was cool this far from the fire and she shivered.

She glared at the now grey abomination wrapped tightly around her. There would be no easy rest with it on, but if she took it off, what would she wear? The style of the dress was revealing, not leaving much room for the usual garments she wore beneath her gowns.

She had two options then; sleep in a filthy gown and sleep poorly or remove the gown and sleep equally poor because she was making herself vulnerable with her nakedness.

That silky blanket would feel so good against her naked skin, though.

Sophia returned to the desk and picked up a letter opener. Even such a simple tool became opulent in Burne's home. The handle was solid gold, making it incredibly heavy, and a row of embedded rubies sparkled along it. She snorted her disdain and palmed the small knife, turning it toward her tight bodice and carefully slicing into the fabric.

A gown was not a letter and the knife was not as proficient as she hoped. Sophia knew there would be no salvaging the dress either way, but she hadn't expected to make such a gory mess of the thing. It was a miracle she didn't stab herself. She had foolishly hoped that she could keep it in good enough condition to tie it back on, even if a little awkwardly.

The damage was done now and there was no going back. She'd have to raid the chest of drawers and armoire tomorrow to see what her options were. Three days wasn't a terribly long time, if she had to wear something foreign. And if Burne was as much a gentleman as he claimed, she would be safe to sleep as she was; naked.

Clutching the gown to her breast as a cover, just in case, Sophia went to the door to search for a lock. There was some kind of mechanism, but after a bit of useless fumbling she decided the better option was to sleep lightly. And with the letter opener beneath her pillow.

When her body sank into the bed, cocooned in silken sheets, Sophia breathed a gratified moan. A comforting smell clung to the fabric, smoke and sandalwood and some other scent she couldn't quite place but knew she wanted to remember. Comfortably resting on her stomach and breathing in that wonderful aroma, Sophia was drowsy and fading from the world in no time.

A soft chuckle was the last noise she made as her heavy eyes succumbed to sleep. What an unbelievably strange day.

CHAPTER 8

BURNE

S OPHIA WAS SLEEPING IN his bed. Burne stood stone still in his doorway, eyes narrowed to slits, watching the gentle rise and fall of her breasts. Her nearly exposed breasts. He hadn't worried when she'd stormed out of the dining hall earlier. There were a great many rooms in this portion of the cave but most were inaccessible. A handful of living quarters and the library were the only doors he knew to be unlocked.

If Sophia had travelled one door further, she would have found a comfortable guest quarter, where Burne planned to keep her for the time being. Fate, it would seem, had no interest in playing games. The dragon had chosen her for a reason. Surely, she was feeling a draw towards him too, no matter how he infuriated her. Even if she avoided him, she sought comfort in his safe haven.

When Burne woke from his half-century slumber, he had no idea why the dragon had awakened. Though this side of him was dominant in most actions, his inner dragon had sway over the more important choices. *Drakonmein* were by no means immortal, but they could extend their lives significantly by falling into a deep, magic induced sleep. If the dragon decided it was time to go dormant, there was nothing he could do to stop it.

The creature would also choose a mate, with or without his say. That was how he unexpectedly came to have a mad woman curled up in his bed—with a letter opener gripped in her palm, he noted with amusement. The instincts of a dragon went beyond the understanding of even the ones who shared a body and soul with them. Burne couldn't figure out how his dragon knew that his mate would be ready for him to claim, but he wouldn't discount it.

That didn't mean he wasn't frustrated with his other half. It wasn't the dragon that would have to woo Sophia. And the dragon didn't seem to care that she should be their enemy. If he was a more hateful man, he would have killed her and returned her to her father drained of all her blood.

The beast stirred inside him, anger rising from his nostrils in a curl of smoke. Poor fool was already smitten with the woman.

"She called you a lizard." Burne pointed out.

His dragon chuffed a dismissal, his attention fixated on Sophia now that he'd made it clear he wasn't tolerating even the thought of harming her. Burne realized his gaze hadn't left her. That porcelain skin, bathed in glorious firelight, made his fingers—and other body parts—twitch. It had to be the softest he would ever touch.

And he would touch it. Just not without her invitation.

Gods, how maddening to want someone so desperately when the only details he knew of her was that she was spoiled, easily angered, and shared blood with the man who destroyed his family.

"You have terrible taste in women." Burne grumbled at the dragon.

Sophia shifted in her sleep, moaning softly. The blanket slipped an inch down her chest, revealing a hint of pink nipple. Heat burned from his neck in both directions, making him unsure if he was blushing or hungering.

The dragon cocked his head with the smuggest expression a reptile was capable of.

"Lizard indeed." Burne muttered, refusing to acknowledge that certain parts of her weren't all that terrible.

She shifted again and he worried Sophia would get the wrong impression if she woke to find him ogling her. Some petty voice in his head wanted to point out that she was in *his* bed, but he realized it wouldn't make her feel any less vulnerable. Quite the opposite. A man could be very territorial over his bed and who he shared it with.

With a sound that was half sigh and half grumble—his bed really was the best of all of them and he was a pinch sore about giving it up—Burne quietly retreated from the room, leaving Sophia to her rest.

His dragon protested mercilessly, very confused as to why Burne wouldn't be joining her. Human courtship and dragon courtship had few similarities. Burne gave an internal speech about respect and mutual desire, noting halfway through that he was talking himself out of going back, at least for one more peek, as much as the dragon.

He gave his head a rough shake and hurried into the guest room adjacent to hers. Once the door was shut, he turned and pressed his palms against the door, bracing himself against the overwhelm of emotions.

Why her? Of all the women in all the kingdoms of Svalta, why did his dragon want her?

She's perfect, he could almost make out the answering words. The dragon couldn't quite talk, but Burne spoke his language fluently. It was the language of their shared soul.

"She's the granddaughter of King George. She shares blood with the man who sought to destroy our kind."

A reptilian shrug was the only response.

"It doesn't bother you? Not even a little?"

She's not guilty of his crimes.

"She worships him like a hero. They had her on that hilltop as a lure for us. To kill us like they killed our namesake."

Bribe. Not lure. This thought seemed to amuse his dragon. As if having a mate would make him hunt less. She was a fire-less human. She needed lots of meat to keep her plump and warm.

"She doesn't want your sheep carcasses."

The beast ignored him, curling in on himself. Burne removed his shirt with an exhale, plopping onto a bed that was not his own and doing the same.

CHAPTER 9

SOPHIA

WARM RAINBOW LIGHT DANCED over Sophia's eyelids. She inhaled several languid breathes, not wanting to wake from this magical dream just yet. The light shimmered like sunlight on a crystalline pool of water. Beneath her, the bed felt softer than it had ever been. And that smell! Where was it coming from? Smoky sandalwood and some unidentifiable spice that was so very faint but still tantalizing as it tickled her nose.

A creaking noise drew the last sweet sleep from her bones. Rosemary coming to wake her. Sophia was one to lounge about in the mornings without a bit of encouragement. When her lids finally lifted, heavy and slow, her sleep stupor evaporated in a rush of panic.

This was not her bed. This was not her room.

The rainbow light she'd been luxuriating in was sunlight pouring through a ceiling made entirely of colorful crystals and gems. It flowed across the chamber walls in intricate geometric patterns, making the most beautiful and unique art she had ever had the chance to admire.

At the foot of the bed, a simple gown made of some shimmery scarlet material was carefully laid out. It too reflected the sunlight, sparkling like dragon scales.

Dragon scales!

All at once she remembered precisely where she was and why. She also remembered that she'd gone to sleep absolutely naked. The fire in the hearth wasn't even a smoldering ember and the air in the stone chamber was cool. Prickles dotted her bare skin, making her uncomfortably aware of her breasts sitting well above the duvet.

Sophia had yet to see a single other person in this castle—or was it a dungeon?—besides Burne. She hoped that somewhere he was hiding his staff. Otherwise it was him who left the gown for her to wear, which meant it was also him who walked in and saw her in her vulnerable state.

He might be a monster, but at least it was of the fantastical sort. Other men might have taken advantage. Sophia could acknowledge that.

He was a decent captor, but a captor, nonetheless.

Sophia was grateful for the simple gown, as it did not require one or more of her handmaids to stitch and cinch her into it. The shimmering material felt like cool water on her skin, a delicious sensation that left her shivering. How was one to stay warm in a home made out of stone? The candles in the hall flickered with an endless glow but emitted no heat.

Didn't reptiles favor warm weather? She could recall seeing snakes sun themselves among garden blooms in summertime. Not once did she witness a serpent stretched out in languid pleasure when the skies were dull and the weather moody.

Sophia laughed at herself. Why was she trying to apply any sort of logic to a man that turned into a dragon? Or maybe a dragon who turned into a man. Whatever he was, it was of the unnatural sort.

A tall, narrow mirror beside the armoire was barely wide enough for her to catch a peek at herself. The dress was beautiful, complimenting the natural color of her lips and drawing a hint of burgundy from her brown hair. Her hair, unfortunately, was not as beautiful as the gown.

Sophia was accustomed to Rosemary's care, spoiled by it, and hadn't considered braiding her frazzled curls before bed.

It would make little difference. Flying Gods knew how far in the palm of a dragon had already tangled it into an impossible mess. She may have to cut it all the way to her skull if someone didn't help her brush it soon. Rosemary would be horrified.

An anxious fear surfaced as she thought of her maid and lifelong friend. Rosemary was the first to mention this so-called revolution to Sophia. How involved was she? When father discovered, she would be severely punished.

Any hint of geniality Sophia thought to offer Burne dissolved. If not for him, she could be home. She could be protecting the people that fought for her, that *wanted* her. She would give anything to know what was happening behind the castle walls.

A knock sprung her focus back to the present. Burne cracked the door with a loud, "are you decent Princess Sophia?"

"Queen." She corrected tersely. "I am a queen."

"Are you?" He leaned on the doorway, arms crossed, handsome face bright with amusement at her expense. "I didn't see you wearing a crown." Then quieter he added, "I didn't see you wearing anything."

Sophia stomped up to him, prodding his chest with her pointer finger. "Tell me your intentions, dragon! Why am I here? Are you so lonely that you kidnap unwilling maidens to keep you company or is this only a twisted game? Where are the others?"

"The others?" Burne deemed only her last question worth answering.

"Surely I can't be the first."

"I assure you, delicate Sophia, that you are my first maiden." Gold sparked at the edge of his eyes. The curve of his lips was not lecherous, but there was a crude quality to it that made prickles of awareness raise on Sophia's skin.

"Do you intend to force me into your bed?"

"I might be a dragon but I'm not a villain." His indignation was genuine. "Think what you will of me, princess. I will prove your accusations false."

"I don't know what you expect me to think, what with you walking into my chambers unannounced this morning."

"My chambers." He purred.

"What?"

"Didn't you know? I don't have to force you into my bed, it seems." He turned on that last smug word, calling over his shoulder. "First we break our fast, then I'll give you a history lesson."

B URNE

The morning spread was as extravagant as the night before. Eggs cooked three different ways, loaves of buttered sweet bread, and a variety of sausages were piled high on platters. There were other breakfast foods in smaller portions, but none made Sophia's eyes glisten the way sticky rolls did. She certainly had a taste for the sweeter things.

And the finer things. Based on the food served per her preferences, she was accustomed to a luxurious lifestyle. Who had eggs served to them in three different ways?

Burne tamped down his judgment. It would serve him well to keep an open mind. She hadn't chosen to be born the granddaughter of a usurper, after all. If George governed his family anything like the kingdoms to the east, the women in his line were given little choice in their daily lives. Perhaps food was Sophia's only indulgence.

"It appears, just like that?" Sophia picked a chunk off a slice of frosted bread and rolled her eyes closed with a moan. Each finger that slipped between her rosy lips to be gently sucked clean was more mesmerizing than the last. Burne had to turn away in order to comprehend the rest of what she said. "What if I have to pass through this room? Will the table fill with my favorite snacks? What happens to the food when we're done? Are there no servants to eat what remains?"

"You are a curious one." He chuckled. "I don't actually know what happens to the food when we're finished, just as I don't know where it comes from. It's possible some poor fellow is sitting down to break his fast now, only to have his food disappear. Or some unsuspecting family might have what's left of a feast dropped into their kitchen from the ether. Magic is inexplicable like that, at least to those of us that do not practice it."

Sophia took a seat, forgetting whatever misgivings she held the prior night and eagerly filling her plate. "Don't you consider what you do magic?"

"I suppose there must be an element of magic involved for it to work." He sat beside her, fascinated that such a willowy woman could eat the quantity of food she served herself. "If there is, I don't use it consciously. I am the dragon. He is me. To move between forms is akin to changing your clothes. I need only think of it."

She chewed thoughtfully. "Do you feel different when you're the dragon? Other than the obvious."

Heat billowed from the place inside of him where the dragon lived. The creature was pleased with her curiosity. *She finds us fascinating.*

She finds us novel. Burne argued.

"I'm in the saddle when I become the dragon, but he is the horse."

"He? You refer to him as if he's not you."

"He is and he's not. We are brothers."

"Who share a body? Like those twins born with their trunks fused together?"

"Is there any topic you filter before you speak it?" Burne scooped a bite of soft boiled eggs.

The question was meant as a tease, but Sophia's expression became shuttered, her eyes dulling. "I am incapable of prudence." It was less self-deprecating and more exasperated. Silent bites passed before she asked, "Why *should* a woman be prudent with her words? My brother is allowed to be bold, even expected to be. He can boast about the girth of his manhood during dinner, and no one is fanning their face in dismay. 'A king's word is law. He speaks it loudly and when he pleases.'" She mimicked a deep voice. "But a princess is demure. 'Seen, not heard.'"

"I would like to hear you, Sophia."

She dropped her fork with a clatter, twisting until her eyes could bore scrutinizing holes into his face. "Do you mock me?"

His pupils shrank, gold burning into his irises. "Never." The breath left his nostrils in a hot flare. "I would never dream of mocking you. Or silencing you."

Oddly, his proclamation did exactly that. Sophia's brows came together in a tight line. She returned to her plate, plucking absent-mindedly at a piece of fruit with no appetite or interest. What had he said wrong? Burne hadn't been in the company of a woman in half a century, but he couldn't recall them being this perplexing.

After their meal, Burne led the way to the library. Sophia trailed behind him, silent and obedient. He hadn't known her long, but already he'd grown accustom to the sound of her unfettered thoughts pouring from her mouth. The stone hallway felt oddly lonely in the absence of her narration.

Upon first discovering her identity, Burne had been angry with his dragon. Of all the women in all the world, why her? Why the offspring of the vilest bloodline to terrorize Calos? Now he was beginning to understand that there was more to a woman than her breeding. Perhaps Sophia Saint George wasn't too marred by leniency and luxury to make a suitable mate.

That all rode on the assumption that if he chose her at the end of their three days, she would choose him too. It would be the shortest courtship in history.

CHAPTER 10

SOPHIA

S OPHIA SHOULD HAVE EXPECTED nothing less than grandeur
when Burne led her into the library. The walls and ceiling were
made in the likeness of the bed chambers. Brilliant colors shimmered
and swam across the stone floor as sunlight dipped in and out of clouds
beyond the ceiling. A hearth the size of a shepherd's cottage housed
a welcoming fire. Luxurious, overstuffed chairs and chaise lounges in
shades of deep green and rich ruby decorated the space.

The room was splendid without giving the impression that it was
curated to flaunt wealth. Whoever built this library had a true passion
for what it housed.

Every inch of wall was lined with massive mahogany bookcases.
Each case was filled nearly to the ceiling with heavy tomes, colorful
novels, and leather journals. It was a wonder the shelves weren't buck-
ling under the weight of so many books.

As a girl, Sophia developed a fondness for books. There was only so
much for a lonely princess to do, so she'd taken up reading. She learned
extensively about matters of state and studied history with eager eyes.
When she wanted to lose herself, she would sprawl on the bearskin rug
by the fire and delve into a fairytale. By the time she was fourteen, her
head was filled with romance and adventure.

Then the king made it clear what her life was to amount to and that
spark of imagination was smothered by loathing and fear. Sophia was

barely a woman grown when she had to steel herself to the reality of her standing as daughter and not son. Dreams of ruling Calos with a loyal, handsome king by her side, revered by subjects who celebrated the new era her rule would bring, were doused.

Sophia fought every match her father tried to make for her and she would have fought for her right to reign, if only she hadn't swallowed the lies she was fed. The people of Calos didn't hate her, as the king claimed, and she should be back home fighting for them right now.

Irritation grew teeth inside her, gnawing away at any interest and patience she had for Burne and his ridiculous bargain. She pivoted, ready to berate him yet again, only to find herself only inches from his broad chest. Heat radiated from him like the warmth that came from the stones of the hearth. His skin smelled smoky, yet an underlying scent of stone and earth made his scent as much cool mountain as it was scorching fire.

For the first time in her life, Sophia felt the words die in her throat. Lizard or not, Burne was beautiful. He was all sharp lines and angles, muscular, long legged, and tall. So very tall. Sophia had to tilt her head back to catch a glimpse of his face.

How did a man come to look gilded? It was as if he was made of the same shimmering scales as his dragon. Would his skin feel as rough too? The tips of her fingers itched to explore. Curious eyes peered back at her, caught between a shade of dragon gold and the muted hazel of a man. He kept his chin proudly lifted, appearing to enjoy her appraisal.

I want to hear you, Sophia.

Once more she found herself wondering why exactly she was here. It wasn't like she was good company. Sophia stepped away from the heady warmth of Burne's body and mustered her most sour expression. It felt wrong on her face. "Well?"

"Well?" His voice was a throaty purr that sent tingles to place she'd never experienced them before.

Sophia swallowed audibly and shuffled further into the center of the room. It was far too hot for a place made of stone. "Why are we here? Did you want me to read you fairytales?"

A muscle in his jaw tightened and softened again, the only show of his frustration. "Quite the opposite. I'd like to show a chapter in my family's history. Our shared family history, actually."

"Dragons keep history?"

"I don't know if you've noticed, but I am as much man as I am dragon. Maybe more so." Again, he managed to make the simple phrase sound seductive.

"I'd like to see it." Why did her voice sound so breathy? And why was she standing so close to him? Hadn't she only just moved away? "The history, I mean. Your family history. It can hardly be ours if only one account is true."

The rich charm was instantly gone, his countenance icy and harsh. "My history is *the* history, princess."

Sophia waved her hand impatiently rather than offering argument.

Burne crossed the room, busying himself with retrieving heavy leather bound books from a shelf Sophia couldn't dream of reaching. She tiptoed in his direction, scanning the book covers from a distance, not trusting herself to be too near him. She might do something as foolish as soothe his anger. Or touch him.

Let him be angry. It was only fair they were both foul and furious.

On its own volition, Sophia's fingertip traced a beautiful seal carved into weathered brown leather. Two dragon heads snaked together, encircled by a ring of fire. She carefully flipped open the book and nearly hissed at the hand scrawled name.

Burne Baxenstone, heir of Calos.

"My grandfather's journal." Burne explained. "He kept one from the time he was a young man. There are a few pages I would have you read, but you are welcome to explore. My family history is—" he smirked; whatever anger he'd been stoking vanished. "—an open book."

"Your charm has already wooed me. Whatever shall I do?" She rolled her eyes until they landed back on the journal.

Burne took a seat at the table, guiding her through the story of his grandparents. The grandparents supposedly murdered by her grandfather. His hand brushed the edge of hers and Sophia nearly jumped away. It felt as if she was too close to a fire, a hair away from burning herself. It was worth it though, to soak the warmth of that fire into her skin.

She brushed her fingers along her hair to clear her head, focusing with all her might on Burne's words and not his rough, scorching hand.

The tale he weaved, citing journal entries and showing her centuries of family lineage, was a tragic one. It was the story of an innocent young woman, born with no rights to land or title, and the rising prince who swept her away. Their romance was a whirlwind, instant passion that brought Burne the first to his knees.

Based on his other entries, Prince Burne was a serious and orderly man. Yet, when it came to Ruby, his bride—or mate as he was known to refer to her—the man waxed poetic. He gushed about her flaxen hair and the shimmer of her blue eyes. An entire page was dedicated to the silky texture of her skin. More than once, Sophia had to press cool palms to her blushing cheeks. The man was besotted.

Burne ascended to the throne the day he was married to Ruby. They reigned nearly two decades before their fates were thrown off course.

A Knight called George McClanahan arrived in Calos on a mission. He intended to kill the dragon that terrorized the kingdom.

Sophia was intimately familiar with this part of the story. George was the son of a wealthy merchant. Not happy to follow in his father's footsteps and claim the family business, young George fought hard to earn knighthood. He was an ambitious man, though, and soon serving as a sword to protect the king of Dunhill was not enough. He craved glory.

That was when he heard tale of a dragon in Calos. The beast blocked out the sky, consuming livestock and sending women and children running for their lives. It was even said that the monster had once swooped down and taken an innocent maiden back to his lair. Brave and self-sacrificing as he was, George set out to liberate Calos from their terror.

"Your grandfather was the dragon? *And* the king?" Sophia scrunched up her nose. "Why did he terrorize his own people?"

Burne's voice boomed in the open space, making her shrink back. "He did not *terrorize* his people. It wasn't long ago that the people of Calos knew the dragons to be their protectors. Why do you think the kingdom is so wealthy? So undisturbed by war and invasion? No one dared to stand against Calos when the king could summon a dragon at will."

Sophia pondered this suggestion. There was talk of raids on the only open border Calos had and she overheard her father dispatching soldiers to handle unknown ships laying anchor on the beaches to the south. Not hearing of such issues of state didn't they mean weren't occurring until recently, however.

Another thought piqued her attention. Most of the suitors father brought to meet her during the warm season did have notable investments in mercenary groups. One plump merchant by the name of Waid bragged about having "an army to rival a king's."

Then again, these suspicions were brought to her attention by the dragon that kidnapped her. It was all terribly convenient for him.

"Yes, how convenient that my family's lineage was steeped in tragedy. How convenient that my throne was stolen by a murderous tyrant. Remind me to thank your grandfather when I meet him in hell." A strange rumbling shook the table. Sophia pressed her palm to the wood, trying to decide if this was another magic housed in Burne's mountain castle or if the roof was about to cave in on them. She followed the tremor to the man sitting across the table. A gasp caught in her throat when her fingertips brushed his chest and found the vibrating noise emanating from there.

"You're doing that?" She looked up to see his eyes golden and reptilian, his features oddly square and skin almost iridescent like scales. "Are you going to kill me?"

It would serve her right. Poking a boring suitor was significantly less risky than poking a man who transformed into a fire breathing dragon.

"Kill you?" The growl made his question gravelly and inhuman. "Why would I kill you?"

"Because I've angered you." Father always warned her that she would earn a violent outburst from a man eventually.

"I wouldn't hurt you, Sophia." Quieter he said, "I couldn't."

"Then why are you," she waved her hand in front of his face, "like that?"

"Because regardless of how I feel about you, I harbor a lifetime of anger toward your family. Your Grandfather was a murdering—"

"And yours was innocent? You mean to tell me he wasn't slaying a shepherd's flock to sate his bestial hunger? Stealing the livelihoods of poor and helpless farmers? Striking fear in the hearts of the people of Calos?"

Burne stood abruptly, the legs of his chair screeching along the stone. "My family has never harmed innocents. We may look the part but we were not the monsters in this story, Sophia. My grandfather took good care of his people. There were not poor and helpless farmers in his time. Unlike your family, he didn't tax the people out of house and home so he could have candied cherries with every meal!"

"Tax the people—oh! I see. This isn't about family lineage, it's about wealth. You think my family luxuriates in finer things while the people starve?" She felt a little sick saying it with such indignation because it was true. The people of Calos were hungry. Anyone sitting at her father's table was not.

"Yes." He paced away and then back. "But this isn't about *my* wealth. It's about injustice. *Saint* George," The word oozed hostility, "murdered my grandfather, attempted to marry his mate against her will to claim the throne, and began a tyrannical reign that left hundreds dead at the hand of their own king. I think my grandfather can be forgiven the loss of a dozen sheep in comparison to that."

"Assuming this is true, how do you know your grandfather was such a pure and righteous ruler? Many believe my grandfather to be a hero, the savior of Calos."

"History is written by the victor, dear princess. The people believe anything your grandfather forced down their throats at sword point."

Sophia crossed her arms and glowered. "You weren't there! How can you believe with such devotion when you weren't even there to witness it yourself?"

"Unbelievable." He tossed his hands over his head. "I have met mules that were less stubborn than you."

"And I have known rabbits with thicker hides than you."

Burne flared his nostrils, eyes shifting between gold and brown at a dizzying rate. Finally, he blew out a breath and muttered, "this was a terrible idea."

"Where are you going?" Sophia called as he retreated from the library.

"To fly."

He was already in the doorway. "What about me? What am I to do?"

"Whatever you please, your highness."

"You only have three days. Are you going to waste one leaving me alone in your library?"

Defeat etched deep grooves in his handsome fac. "Yes, I am."

CHAPTER 11

SOPHIA

SOPHIA WAS ABSOLUTELY NOT going to feel guilty. Guilt implied she was in the wrong. She was a captive, a victim. Guilt was not her burden to bear in this mess. It *was* possible that she pushed too hard, as she was known to do. Only because she hated the idea of being associated by blood with a tyrant and a murderer.

And yet...she was, wasn't she? Everyone knew King George was a tyrant, even if they feared speaking it aloud. Her father was better than her grandfather, but the echoes of George's rule were present in Calos to this day.

A murderer, though? Was a man a murderer when he killed an enemy on the battlefield? Sophia thought not. It was clear to her now that the dragon was more than a mere beast, but that didn't mean her grandfather was wrong to slay him.

The argument felt callous and weak.

"Gods damn it all." Sophia kicked the nearest chair leg, wincing when her toes bent at an awkward angle. Why was she so wrapped in tension?

*Because I've been kidnapped by a lizard man. A distractingly hand-some and **almost** charming lizard man who claims every story I've been told about my family is a lie.*

Truthfully, Sophia didn't have a good reason to defend her lineage. She was well aware of George's faults and she disagreed vehemently with many of her father's political choices. She'd heard the accounts from handmaids and kitchen girls of poverty and famine.

On the outside Calos appeared wealthy. On the streets, men in rags begged for crumbs to feed their family. Shepherds were required to sell their entire flocks to cover debts. Widowed mothers were forced into prostitution to keep their children sheltered and warm.

Still, she struggled with the idea that her grandfather was a usurper and not crowned king by marriage. Except... there was the tale of his first wife. What was the woman's name? She'd been heir to the throne but she died before they produced any children.

No, she hadn't simply *died*. The queen ended her own life.

The fire in the hearth shrank to half its size and Burne showed no sign of return. More bored than frustrated, Sophia decided to delve deeper into Burne's family history. There was no harm in reading, even if it was false.

What were once hopeful, even romantic, journal entries became dark and hateful when the name George of house Mclanahan appeared on the page.

"He's taken my Ruby. My only true treasure."

Sophia read on with bated breath, her heart racing as she felt immersed in the recounting.

"It has come to this, as I feared it would. I will do what I must. My crown, my kingdom, and all of its riches, my people, my throne, and the blood in my veins, I shed it all for Ruby."

Sophia stared at the very last entry made in the journal, wiping beneath her eye before a tear could escape. The writing, normally neat and legible, was sloppy and rushed. She didn't doubt the emotion poured onto those pages for a single moment. How could she?

Feeling unsettled and suddenly riddled with doubts, she carefully closed the journal and pushed it away. She considered leaving the library and hunting down the dining hall. With the right thought maybe the magic table would summon candied cherries and orange glazed scones. Sophia could drown her confusion and the odd sorrow eating away at her heart with sweets.

Burne's comment about her family luxuriating in gluttonous meals echoed in her mind, souring her appetite and her mood in one go.

Another portion of afternoon was wasted pacing the library. Once or twice she picked up novels of fantasy and romance but found she couldn't muster the enthusiasm for such things. Eventually the fire dimmed and the air in the stony space chilled. The silky dress Burne adorned her in was beautiful but did nothing to keep ice from crystallizing in her joints.

She searched and searched but found no wood to keep the fire fed. Finally, she gave up and made a hurried journey back to the sleeping quarters. Not before taking the books Burne laid out on the table, of course.

Sophia could be called many unkind names. Coward would never be one of them. The story, whether fact or fiction, was unfinished. It was obvious what happened to Burne's grandfather. He was a dragon and Saint George was famous for slaying him. What was Ruby's fate?

A niggling suspicion picked at her the entire walk down the long stone hall. The story of her grandfather's first wife was replaying in her head, creating a growing sense of dread.

Sophia paused at the entrance to the chamber she'd slept in the night before. Burne's chamber. Her fingers brushed the golden handle, her skin as cool as the metal.

Why had she returned here? Why hadn't she requested he place her in another room?

He wasn't around for that request now. There were other doors. She could try them all until she found one that was unlocked, even if it wasn't a bedroom. But she was freezing and the massive bed was comforting and warm. What was the harm in utilizing the bed? It was daytime and it wasn't like he would join her in it.

Justification after justification played out until she was sprawled across the mattress, a feather filled blanket covering her icy body. She forgot what she'd been arguing with herself over when a smoky scent curled into her nostrils. Instantly her body relaxed, the buzz of anxiety drowned out by the unusual peace that settled over her. Now that she knew the bed to be Burne's, she could detect the masculine scent that mingled with smoke and spice.

Oh Gods. She was smelling his pillow! What in the heavens was wrong with her?

Sophia bolted upright, scrambling from the bed as if it were ablaze. *She* felt ablaze. Sparks climbed from up her arms and legs, converging in her chest and...lower. She raked her nails down her arms in an attempt to dislodge the unsettling sensation.

When the heat finally dissipated, it left a previously unknown place within her empty. Sophia was lonely. And why wouldn't she be? She'd gone from a castle that constantly buzzed with life to a stone prison. A beautiful prison, but still a prison.

Though, she supposed, she was a captive in both.

The stack of books stared at her from the bedside table. Was Ruby a captive in that same castle Sophia called home? A caste built by Burne's forefathers?

Gripping the next book in the stack to her chest—a ledger of family lineage—Sophia shivered her way to the hearth. She wasn't as skilled in fire starting as she should have been. Rosemary made it look easy. The flint was stubborn and didn't give Sophia a spark until her hands were raw and her fingers scraped. When it did, she realized the sparks were not strong enough to catch an entire log.

After finally gathering enough kindling and blowing life into what she thought was a very impressive fire, Sophia plunked down onto the plush fur rug before the hearth and flipped to a random page in the ledger. Unlike Burne Sr.'s diary, the family lineage was relatively boring. She supposed it was interesting *objectively* because it traced the bloodline of men who could turn into dragons.

That didn't mean she was personally invested in King Ardal and his nine sons. For dragon men, they led rather unimaginative lives. Sophia may as well be reading her own family history. The only difference was that the marriages—matings as they were often referred to in the book—were between common women and royal men. It was not a practice she'd seen before.

It wasn't until Sophia reached one of the very last pages in the book that her pulse began drumming.

Burne Baxenstone, the only son of Canmore and heir to the throne of Calos, was betrothed to Ruby Smythe at the festival of the dragon's heart. They married three weeks later outside the city walls. All of Calos was in attendance.

Sophia scanned the page, searching for any mention of her grandfather. There were several other royal lines mentioned as well as three family names that appeared to be other dragon men. Was it that common? How was it possible that dragons had soared through the skies of the realm for so many centuries and no one discovered their secret? Or had the people simply forgotten, as people were like to do?

She gingerly flipped the aged page, praying that what she anticipated was wrong. Two black X's marked Burne and Ruby's line, a glaring break in the family tree. Sophia traced the marks with her finger, following the broken line below Ruby and Burne's two children.

There he was. Burne the second, named for his grandfather. The last living member of the Baxenstone line.

Those two marks became daggers in Sophia's heart when she finally found the words she so desperately hoped would not be there.

King Burne Baxenstone, slain by the usurper George Mclanahan. Survived by Queen Ruby, one son, and two daughters.

Queen Ruby, killed in a fall from the tower of the queen.

An image conjured in Sophia's mind of a beautiful woman in a white bridal gown, a red sash painted across her middle as blood spilled from the place where her body cracked open upon impact. The visage was vivid in her mind, the gory end to a terrible tale whispered to her by Rosemary when she was just a girl.

"Why can't I play in the queen's tower?" Sophia had whined. "I want to see Calos from the highest window."

"That place is cursed." Rosemary warned. "It has been since your grandfather's first wife threw herself from the window."

In a world ruled by mischievous Gods, a world where men could shift into fire breathing monsters, it was hard to believe in coincidence. Sophia was afraid that this was not one.

CHAPTER 12

BURNE

THE SUN WAS SETTING when Burne returned to the hidden entrance to his family home. He tucked his massive wings, rocketing his body through the narrow stone passage and landing gracefully in the main hall. Blade-like claws flexed into the rock beneath him, leaving scratches on the smooth surface. His dragon had allowed him a period of grace, taking the afternoon to compose himself and work the anger out of his system. Now the beast was frustrated and restless.

They'd left Sophia alone for too long. What if she needed something? What if being alone frightened her? What if she tried to leave?

Logically Burne knew she couldn't get far—if she could find her way out at all—but he couldn't shake the image of her tumbling down the mountainside, palms scraped, bare feet bleeding from the stone. She wasn't exactly equipped for travel the last time he saw her.

The muscles in his shoulders ached as they reformed from leathery wings to the ordinary flesh of a man. Burne rolled them uselessly, shifting his neck back and forth to ease the tension that still remained there. He hurriedly dressed in the simple wool pants and shirt he left behind that morning, not bothering with shoes. The cool stone relieved some of the excess heat his body carried when he was agitated.

Thunder rumbled in his gut as he made his way to the dining hall. Not wanting to be bothered by the dramatic reaction of horrified people spying him in the sky, Burne had opted to go southwest in his flight. He'd spent the afternoon admiring the glittering sunshine reflecting on turquoise waters, skimming the whitecaps with the tips of his talons and tasting the sea spray that splashed up from the force of his beating wings. The coast was a stunning sight, a place that always relaxed him, but there was nothing to eat.

Not unless he wanted to behave like a common bird, diving for fish. His dragon shuddered at the idea. He was much fonder of red meat than seafood.

The mouthwatering aromas of a magically prepared feast were absent when he entered the dining hall. He thought perhaps it was only indication that Sophia hadn't made her way there yet, either waiting for him or not feeling welcome to help herself to a meal. Guilt churned like the ocean waves whose scent still lingered on his sun kissed skin. Burne should never have left her alone for so long.

Those internal waves crashed painfully into him—or was that the claws of his dragon?— when he spotted the princess huddled meekly at the far end of the table, a teacup clutched between her lithe hands. Her dark hair was spilling over her face and shoulders like a curled mass of chestnut colored vines. The pallor of her skin was unhealthy, grey and lacking that creamy smoothness it had this morning. Rings rimmed her eyes, giving them a haunted edge and robbing them of the sparkle that so reminded him of the coastal waters he admired earlier.

What happened to her in the hours that he was gone? Was she hurt? Ill?

"Sophia?" She jumped at the sound of her name, nearly spilling the tea cradled in her palms. The lines around her eyes darkened further as she squinted angrily at him. At least that much hadn't changed.

"Where have you been?" She straightened, lifting her chin in an attempt at composure.

"The coast."

"The coast?" That pert chin dipped, nearly to the table. "How did you get there?"

"I flew."

Disbelief slowly eased into realization. "Of course. How could I forget you're a flying lizard?"

The blood left his fingers as he clenched and unclenched his fists. How did she manage to be so beautiful and so prickly all at once? "Are you unwell?"

"Does it matter? "She sniped back. "Afraid I'll make you ill when you finally devour me?"

"Gods woman, what is the matter with you?" Burne slapped his palm against the tabletop. "I don't plan to eat you, torture you, or violate you. Would it kill you to be diplomatic?"

Sophia cocked her head, gaze slanted upward as she considered. "Yes."

"At least you're honest."

"That makes one of us."

"What malicious act have I committed that unendears me to you?"

"Besides kidnapping me?" She pushed her cup of tea away so hard it sloshed over the side. "You've harassed the people of Calos—*my* people—for half a year. They live in constant fear!"

The barely bridled rage that Burne spent the afternoon quelling resurfaced, bubbling like an overheated volcano. The porcelain teacup shattered as the back of his hand swiped it furiously across the table. "They wouldn't have to be afraid if they were still *my* people!"

Sophia's ardor washed her cheeks in a rosy tint, but it was quickly painted over by the unsettling pale. Her tone was soft, almost sad, when she said, "If only I could change the past. Then perhaps you wouldn't punish me for sins I hadn't even known my family committed."

He inhaled slowly, lowering himself to the bench beside her. "Tell me what's troubling you, Sophia."

"Where should I begin?" She sighed and rested her forehead on the backs of her hands. "There is a tower in the south wing. We call it the queen's tower." When she lifted her dark eyes back to his, they were unfocused, distant. "I've never been inside. No one has. My grandfather had the staircase destroyed and the door barricaded."

"Do you know why?" Burne did and it made the appetite plummet from his stomach.

"It's haunted. Cursed, some say." Sophia swallowed and averted her gaze. "My grandfather's first wife was a very sad woman. She—" Delicate fingertips pattered on the tabletop as she grappled with the words. "She threw herself from the window at the top of the tower." The confusion and distress dug deeper into the angles of her face. "She was your grandmother, wasn't she? Ruby?"

"Yes."

"And she wasn't a willing wife, was she?"

He shook his head. "She was never his wife at all. Your grandfather seized the throne upon her death, forging the marital contract that she refused to sign. There was no one to oppose his right to rule but my father and he was grieving, afraid for his family." The calluses on his palms scraped against the growing scruff on his chin. "Before his death, he admitted that he never wanted to be king. Losing his parents devastated him, but losing the throne liberated him. If only he'd realized how the death of my grandfather would devastate the people too."

"I don't...It's just...there is so much I don't understand. So much I'm not sure I believe." Sophia pinched her bottom lip with blunt teeth. "I never knew my grandfather, but many in Calos revere him. His praises are sung as a hero who saved the kingdom. I'm expected to believe he was a murderer? A usurper who tried to force a grieving widow into a marriage?"

"I can't expect you to believe anything." Burne gently touched her forearm. "But it's the truth. I gain nothing from lying to you."

"If my father wasn't set in his antiquated ways, he wouldn't have named my brother heir. I would inherit the throne. And if you led me to believe it wasn't rightfully mine, I would step down and allow you to reclaim your family title. That's quite a lot to gain." She glared at the hand on her arm and shifted away.

He spoke softly, barely daring to let her hear. "Whether you or I were heir to the throne, you would be queen."

"What do you mean by that?" The ice returned to her tone, so thick the air grew frosty.

Burne brushed her question aside, countering with, "have you heard your grandfather's other name? He deemed himself a Saint and is called 'hero' by those who are too young to remember, but do you know the history of his rule?"

That swallowed her indignation. "They called him *The Flesher King*."

"Do you know why?"

"He made blood sacrifices to the Gods."

"Those are only the worst of his crimes. Your grandfather was a tyrant, your father only so removed from those sacrilegious and violent ways" He straddled the wooden bench, facing her. "It isn't my wish to cause you pain, Sophia, nor am I telling you this to coerce you. My only desire is for you to understand, for you to see history in the light of truth."

"Your history is not the same as mine."

"History is always written by the victorious party, princess." He repeated his words from before, gentler.

Sophia sighed tiredly, her expression falling from suspicious to weary. Quiet heartbeats passed between them, her wandering deep in her thoughts and him desperately curious about her journey. The silence was ruptured by the belligerent groan of his stomach. Dragons had enormous appetites and he would soon be paying for his lack of sustenance.

Laughter followed his complaining gut, so unexpected that he stood from the table, posture defensive. Heat flared across his pupils and he felt them narrowing, the world becoming duller through the eyes of a dragon. The surrounding hall was dark, shades of grey, except for the beautiful yellow-red aura that glowed around Sophia.

"Do you always do that when you're scared?" She chortled, pointing to his eyes.

"I wasn't scared." He huffed, his breath creating a puff of steam around him. "I was protecting you."

"My valiant lizard savior." Her giggling continued behind her palm. "If you're so hungry, why don't you eat me already?"

This time the heat that seeped into him was much lower than his eyes. Burne wanted nothing more than to devour the teasing smile from her lips. For the first time, he caught himself—not the dragon but *him*—looking at her without judgement. She could be the granddaughter of the wealthiest, most powerful king, or even the daughter of a god, and here it didn't matter. In the confines of his stone home, she was only a woman and him only a man.

Burne was never more aware of being a man. Her womanhood was pronounced, too. The shimmering red fabric of her gown molded to the round of her breasts as she leaned over the table. The way she was seated pulled the dress tight to her legs, leaving very little of her hips and thighs for him to imagine. His fingertips itched to sink into that supple flesh.

"What would you like?" Did her voice sound sultry or was he imagining it?

He gulped. "What would I like?"

"To eat." The grin that twisted her lips was wicked. "You're at my mercy now."

I have been at your mercy from the moment I laid eyes on you.

Burne took the seat beside her, propping his elbows on the table and smiling. "What's your favorite type of roast?"

CHAPTER 13

SOPHIA

"Y OU HAVE NO KITCHEN for a cook, no servants to bring you meals...who keeps the dust away? Launders your clothing?" Sophia grimaced on the next question, knowing that she was in dire need of one. "What about a bath?"

"We've never had servants." Burne licked grease from his fingers. He'd been so ravenous upon his return that he devoured four roasts with his bare hands. Sophia had to admit, she appreciated his behavior. At least here there were no expectations—no etiquettes to be hounded about, no fine clothes to fuss over. With just the two of them, they could act as they pleased.

Which was why she finished her own dinner with her fingers, covering her already filthy skin in another layer to be scrubbed away.

"I didn't encounter clouds of dust while I browsed your library." She pinched a biscuit crumb between her fingers and ate it. "Are you going to tell me the whole place is kept with magic?"

He shrugged. "Many generations of my family took this place as their home and sanctuary before me. Who is to say just how much magic lives in these old stone walls?"

"If I wish to be clean, do I simply close my eyes and imagine it so, the way I did dinner?"

"There is a bathhouse, of sorts." Veins of gold seeped into his irises before he blinked them away again. "You'll need my help."

"Ha!" She slapped the table. "That is a new one. I may be a princess but I am not so helpless I can't bathe myself."

"The water is cold. It's fed by a spring deep within the mountain. You will need me to heat it."

"Heat the water and leave me to it then." Sophia stood, more than eager to soak away the last two days. Had it been two already? Was she already closer to the end of this arrangement? Unexpected disappointment skittered along her sternum. She squashed it like a beetle in her pumpkin patch. Burne was her captor. Not her friend, her *captor*.

There should be no need to remind herself of that. One peaceful dinner didn't equate to good rapport. The story about his family history was compelling and perhaps there were aspects of it that held truth. Just as Sophia's family history contained truths and exaggerations. That didn't mean Burne was trustworthy. He wanted her throne—well, her brother's throne. That much was clear.

What would he do to gain—or regain, according to him—his family legacy? Sophia was acutely aware of the leverage she made. The leverage she would make, anyway, if her father cared for her beyond her ability to win him a worthy marriage contract. That was *before* half the kingdom stood in support of her as he tried to sacrifice her to a dragon.

Again, she paused her thoughts, shocked that it was only yesterday morning when her father announced his plans for her. Time stretched oddly in this stone place. Sunlight filtered through the many gems and crystals that decorated the ceiling but it was muted, making it difficult to tell dawn from dusk. Being entrenched in stone should be suffocated. The whole place should feel like a tomb.

That was the last word Sophia would use to describe it though. *Sanctuary* was the name that softly whispered through her mind. Here, time was frozen. The days passed unnoticed, and the world could be forgotten. All her wants, her fears, her uncertainties about her future in Calos when she returned, were quieter now. They still lived in the back of her mind, but they were no longer a constant irritant, buzzing and growing the way an overactive beehive did.

Burne allowed her to ruminate undisturbed as he led her away from the dining hall. They passed the doors to the many bed chambers, heading in the direction of the library. A sharp turn took them another way, following a narrow, shadowed corridor that Sophia hadn't seen during their earlier expedition. The enchanted fires that burned endlessly in the halls vanished. Beneath her feet the floor began to slant, throwing her off balance in the dark.

The beat of her pulse quickened and she remembered her earlier lecture about trust. Burne did not have hers and it was never more apparent than in this dark, damp tunnel. Foreboding rooted her feet in place. A man who could turn into a dragon had no need for dungeons and torture chambers. Why use all manner of devious devices on your victim when you could become a giant lizard and devour them whole?

Still, Sophia couldn't shake the apprehension tickling down her legs, keeping her from following him further.

"Sophia?" Scorching gold eyes turned on her, brilliant lights in the thickening darkness. "I'm sorry."

"For what?" Damn the quaver in her voice.

"I've forgotten you can't see." His face became clear before her as he returned, reaching out and taking her hand. His was warm, engulfing hers, and relief left her chest in a swift breath. There was a smile in his voice, though she couldn't quite see it. "My mother was always complaining about this hall. She swore she would break her neck. The stone becomes slick from the steam. It can be rather treacherous for a woman."

Now Sophia was a touch offended. "Oh? Are women incapable of being surefooted?"

"Human." He corrected. "The women in my family are all human." His fingers squeezed, tugging her toward him. "Come along, my mulish princess. I'll protect you."

The temptation to kick his backside and send him tumbling was difficult to resist.

Each and every room in Burne's strange castle had surprised her, leaving her speechless with awe. Even in their unique beauty, none of them could compare to the cavern that opened up before them. The simplicity of the room—if one could even call it that—was a stark contrast to the chambers above. In fact, Sophia wasn't sure that she would recognize this place as an intentional living space if she'd stumbled upon it.

Burne's bathhouse, as he called it, was an ordinary cave. Or it would be if not for the enchantment that lit the space. Thousands of blue specks glittered along the ceiling, the stars come to life on a canvas of stone. Crystalline droplets hung from stalactites, dripping lazily into the pool below. The water was the purest Sophia had ever seen, so translucent that it appeared to be a gently moving blanket of electric blue lights.

"This..." Rarely did she find herself grappling for words. "It's...how? What enchantress can create such a work of art?"

"The Gods."

Sophia arched a brow. "The Gods gifted your family a bathhouse? I've opened my mind quite a bit for you, Burne of Baxenstone, but that doesn't make me gullible."

His laughter echoed around the enclosed space, thrumming along her skin until she shivered. The sound was pleasant, untouched the hostility that hung darkly over their previous interactions. Sophia had a sudden urge to make a fool of herself, anything to summon more joy from him.

Stupid. She chided herself. *Do not lose your wits because of a handsome lizard.*

"The Gods created this place for their own glory. My ancestors discovered it when they claimed the rest of the cave as their home."

"This is natural?" Sophia brushed her fingers along the glowing wall. They came back damp but clean. "What is it?"

He lifted his shoulders. "I don't know. Something that grows in the dark. Perhaps an algae." Burne mirrored her, running his hand along the stone and admired the way the luminous blue danced beneath his palm. "Or perhaps it is magic. You believe in magic, don't you, princess?"

"If you asked me a year ago, my answer would have been a resounding 'no.'" She walked to the edge of the pool, staring through the water to study the bottom. "I wanted it to be real, as childish as that sounds. As a girl I did little else but read books about magic, about enchantresses and fairies, about *dragons.*" She glanced over her shoulder. His eyes were alight, pupils between human and the narrow slits of the dragon. They sparkled brighter than the entire cavern, twin pools of liquid gold.

"I didn't know princesses read books."

"We aren't all illiterate twits."

"Do you take every comment so personally?" Burne dipped his barefoot in the water, splashing it up toward her. She squealed and scurried away. "I meant, I hadn't realized princesses had time for reading. I imagine you were busy keeping court, entertaining ladies, that sort of thing."

"Your imagination is inaccurate. I can't speak for other princesses, but I have never entertained ladies."

"Why not?"

Sophia bit her lip, suddenly feeling self-conscious. Would Burne view her differently if he knew how hated she was? The scorn of fellow girls at court burned when she was a child, but she hardened herself to it quick enough. What did it matter if a bunch of nitwits were uninterested in her? Sophia had no desire to play their trivial games anyway. Why pretend to be queen if the sole purpose of the game was to act as a *wife*, not a ruler?

Perhaps that rejection wounded her more than she had previously been willing to admit to herself. Or perhaps it was only the shame of it that kept her tightlipped now, skirting around the pool until she'd put it between them.

"That is an answer you will have to earn."

"Ah, I live for a good challenge."

"Then you must love me." She knelt beside the water, skimming fingers over the surface. "Gods!" Sophia gasped. "It's frigid. How do you heat it?"

She jumped when his voice came from directly behind her. "I'll show you."

Burne's hands slipped beneath the water. She watched, anticipating some obvious sign of magic. Was he going to breathe fire? Any excitement seemed ridiculous when a minute ticked by without even a spark. When he lifted his hands, water cupped between them, Sophia was unimpressed. "Don't make that face." He chided. "Touch it."

Sophia dipped two skeptical fingers into the water dripping down from his hands, eyes widening when she realized there was *steam* floating above it. "You can warm water by touching it?"

"I can warm anything by touching it." It was another double entendre. She felt that warmth he promised in places a maiden shouldn't be familiar with. Was that his game? Win her trust so that he could seduce her? To what end?

"I'm not your path to the throne."

Bewilderment twisted his features, his frown a harsh shadow over his bright eyes. "What?"

"If you wish to take the throne of Calos," said Sophia, feeling an odd pang at the words she was about to speak. "Then you are wasting your time with me."

"Take off your clothes."

"What?" Now she was the one struck with bewilderment.

"I'm not entertaining your suspicions any longer. If you want to take a bath, you'll have to undress yourself."

She stuck her chin out at a stubborn angle. "Not in front of you."

"Then you can take a cold bath." Burne tossed his head back, an exasperated noise that tapered off into a rumbling growl. "Offer me a modicum of your faith, Sophia. I'm not some lecher, otherwise I could have taken advantage of your situation long before now."

Sophia regarded him warily. The point he made was a fair one, though she refused to admit as much aloud. Still, she needed to keep her wits about her. It would be too easy to be wooed by his golden skin and that beguiling smile. A lecher he might not be, but his innuendos made it clear enough what he desired from her. At the end of the day, it was what all men desired of a woman.

"Turn your back."

"I will avert my eyes but I need contact with the water."

"Fine." She stuck her lip out, tugging heatedly at the straps of her dress until they slipped from her shoulders.

Burne did as he promised, lifting his gaze to the ceiling, his legs tossed over the side of the pool so his calves soaked in it. Sophia took several paces away from him before lowering herself to the stone edge.

The air was damp and cool against her skin, the stone icy. Goosebumps made slow waves up her arms, echoing the subtle waves that disturbed the surface of the water.

"I'll be watching you." She told Burne, dipping one foot into the water. It wasn't quite a hot bath but it was warm enough. Sophia didn't understand how his magic worked, but the pool seemed rather large for anyone to heat without flames.

"And I won't be watching you." He blew out a breath, muttering, "regrettably."

The temperature seemed to increase by the time she was navel deep in the pool. The floor beneath her feet had a slight incline, making the edges of the pool shallower. It disappeared from beneath her feet when she reached the middle, leaving her floating. Ducking her head underwater, Sophia squeezed her eyes shut, enjoying the increasing heat. How did he do it without flames? Were parts of him still a dragon, even when he took the shape of a man?

She broke the surface with a gasp, having held her breath as long as she was capable. Burne's disgruntled voice called, "Please refrain from drowning yourself, unless your intention is to lure me into the water to rescue you."

"Wouldn't that please you?" She teased, splashing fat droplets of water in his direction.

Another growl rebounded oddly off the walls. Somehow, she understood this one was less frustration and more playful.

"I can swim, you know." She raked fingers through her hair, untangling it as best she could. Soot and dust seeped from her, creating a cloud in the water around her.

"Rosemary taught me. On the hottest summer nights, she helped me sneak through the kitchen. We swam in the pond beyond the flower gardens." Rivulets of water ran down her temples, reminding her of those fond memories. "Sometimes, if the moon was new and the night especially dark, we swam naked."

"You are the most delinquent princess I've ever known."

"I imagine I'm the only princess you've ever known."

"Indeed." He chuckled. "Who is Rosemary?"

"The closest I have to a mother." Her smile was affectionate but the worry that lumped on the back of her throat was bitter. What happened to Rosemary after Burne took Sophia away? Did father discover her role in the short lived rebellion?

Before she could stop herself, Sophia was rambling to Burne about Rosemary, telling him of her animated bedtime stories and the time she fearlessly caught a mouse with her bare hands and tossed it out the window. When Sophia was a rambunctious child, climbing trees and taking sharp turns around rose bushes in a game of chase with her brother, Rosemary expertly stitched the many tears in her gowns so father wouldn't be angry. She worked hard, her hands bony and calloused, and her days were often long, but she never acted resentful towards Sophia.

Sophia knew Rosemary wished for more time with her son. He was only two years older than Sophia and had often been left to tend to their sheep as a boy so Rosemary could earn her wages working in the castle. A perennial regret was planted in those stories, it's roots thick and sturdy from years of growth. Sophia wished she had done more for Rosemary. The poor woman was scarcely a wife before she was a widow, alone with a young son and a farm she couldn't possibly manage on her own.

If ever Sophia became a mother, she hoped to be half as strong in character as Rosemary. The best qualities—perhaps all of her good qualities—were gifted to her by that woman.

"You're worried for her." Burne observed.

"She tried to secret me away." Steam rose up between them, the water now warm enough to make Sophia's muscles pliable. She was reclined, letting the water hold her while the heat soaked into her bones. "I half suspect she was the one who started the whole rebellion. She is careful, but that doesn't make her soft. Maybe Rosemary should rule Calos instead of some pigheaded royalty."

"Pigheaded?" Burne kicked his legs to splash her. "Speak for yourself."

More silence billowed around them like steam, comfortable and soothing. Sophia couldn't remember the last time she felt so at peace. Life as a princess was luxurious, that much was undeniably. She was painfully aware of the lavish abundance her family reveled in while the people of Calos went hungry. That didn't mean she was happy.

There was no safety for the daughter of a king, not really. From the moment she became a woman, Sophia was thrust into the world of courtship. Father had once called her a treasure. Young, naive Sophia thought it a compliment. The woman she'd grown into realized that he wasn't doting on her, he was counting his coins.

Calos had seen better economic times than many kingdoms. The wealth of their mountain home was known around the world. Dragons, it would seem, were better managers of gold. Money disappeared much faster than it ever arrived during her family's reign. Sophia had only been made aware of how dire the situation was when she was suddenly trotted in front of half a dozen foreign suitors every fortnight, suitors that had fat purses or guaranteed trade routes across the sea.

That was when Sophia learned to protect herself with her sharp mouth. Rosemary once joked that they couldn't find a wet nurse that would feed Sophia as a babe because she was born with a barbed tongue. It was true that she had little qualms about speaking her mind.

She merely had to hone that particular trait to frighten off potential husbands.

She'd been lucky. Most of her suitors were old, plenty on their second—or third or fourth—wife and looking for an easy woman. A woman who wanted their wealth enough to submit like a puppy, coming to their beds when they called, perching prettily at their feet. Sophia would throw herself from a window before marrying a man who expected docility from her.

And suddenly her mood dropped. Oh, what a poor choice of words. The image of Ruby tumbling from the queen's tower, heartbroken and afraid for her children, played through her mind as a waking nightmare. What had her grandfather done to the poor woman? To her family?

"Are you alright, love?" Burne's legs splashed restlessly in the water, his words strained.

Was he breaking his oath and looking at her? Sophia hadn't thought herself shy but the fear made her arms curl protectively over her breasts. It wasn't exactly modesty that had her covering herself. She felt she needed a shield, some way to guard her wayward body from warming at the mere idea of his gaze on her.

The strain snapped taut, startling her. "Sophia?"

"I'm fine." She slowly unfurled from her coiled position, raising her eyes to find he was still doing the same. "Why did you think something was wrong?"

"Your heartbeat changed suddenly."

"You can hear my heart beating?"

Burne tapped the side of his ear. "Dragons have good hearing. It's useful for hunting."

"Are you hunting me?"

"No." The answer was abrupt, the sudden brightness of his eyes belying a different truth. Gold clashed with brown, like two beams of sunlight had broken through the cave walls. "I can't help but hear the noises around me. I heard you talking in your sleep down the hall."

"I don't talk in my sleep."

"Do so."

"I have nothing to wear." She gripped the stone edge of the pool, belatedly realizing that if she climbed out, she would be forced to put the same dress back on, wet.

"I can remedy that, but you'll have to wear the dress you started in, for now." Burne hummed. "Unless you'd rather air dry."

"Wolf." Sophia hoisted herself out of the water, shoving his shoulder with her bare foot. It wasn't enough force to topple him into the pool, but she was tempted.

"Dragon." He corrected, standing and walking back to the narrow passage that led to the upper chambers. He waited as she wiggled awkwardly into her dress. "Come along, princess."

She took his offered hand—too eagerly, perhaps—and let him lead her up the stone incline and down the hallway that housed the bed chambers. They stopped at a door three down from hers—well, Burne's. It was only when he dropped her hand to fiddle with the lock that she realized he was still holding it.

Sconces with no visible fuel ignited on the walls as Burne pushed open the door. Even with the magical lighting, the room was dull. Trunks and covered paintings were placed haphazardly around the space, blocking the path to the few pieces of furniture visible from the doorway.

"There are more dresses than a woman could ever need in here." He gestured vaguely to several trunks and a wardrobe peeking out from behind a covered chair. "Pick what suits you."

Sophia opened the first trunk within reach, coughing as a thin puff of dust emerged. Apparently, some of this place was left uncared for, magic or not. Inside the trunk was a garment so old and antiquated that she would see it in a museum sooner than she would try to fit herself into it. The next trunk had less dated dresses but there were so many straps and ties she would never get into on her own.

"Where did you find this one?" She motioned to the wet dress clinging to her skin.

Burne took a languid look over the dress, lingering in places she was fairly certain the fabric was outlining more than a man should see of a maiden. He licked his lips and Sophia ignited the way the sconces had moments ago. Warmth was pumping rapidly through her veins, gathering below her navel and making her uncomfortably aware of her nakedness beneath the thin dress. What was this feeling and how did he inspire it so easily?

Gods, how could he not? It had to be innate, something any woman would feel when she saw the man. His simple wool clothes were unimpressive, the pants rolled halfway up to his knees, but they outlined the lean, muscular frame Sophia knew was hiding beneath them. Though he lived in a windowless home built of stone, his skin was the same golden shade as a farmer's, sun kissed and flawlessly smooth. That tousled head of dark blonde hair was the perfect match, reminding her of a man who was born on the coast, not in a cave.

Even those features could be ignored if she focused enough. It was his eyes that had her captivated, flickering between shades of gold, pupils dilating not like a man's but a dragon's. She loved the sensation that tickled across her skin when those eyes were upon her. No gaze had ever felt tangible before, not without inciting disgust. Though Sophia was sure the fire that burned in his irises was lust, she didn't despise him for it. Burne had been truthful when he promised he was not a lecherous man.

And she saw it. Whatever desires were fueling him went deeper than anything so base and fleshly. Eyes shouldn't be able to speak more than tongues, but Sophia felt as if she was hearing his thoughts, a thousand unspoken wishes travelling from the windows to his soul.

Gods, his lips were captivating, too.

Why was he standing so close to her? Or was it she standing close to him? His nearness made her feel as if she was beside a bed of coals; almost too hot to be comfortable yet pleasing in a way that made her wish she could touch them, could take their heat inside of her.

"Dress." Sophia blurted, stumbling backward until she hit a trunk. "I need a dry dress."

The movement of his throat as he swallowed was mesmerizing. "Dress." He echoed.

She nodded vehemently. "Yes."

"There." He pointed to a trunk to her right, turning his back to her, hands roughing up the sides of his face.

Sophia yanked the first decent looking scrap of fabric from the trunk, scurrying to the doorway with it clutched in her fist. A glance over her shoulder proved to be a terrible idea. Burne was watching her again, his eyes reflecting the lie he told earlier. She spent enough time watching the kitchen cats chasing the mice that pilfered grains from the pantry to know the look of a beast on the hunt. He took one prowling step toward her, then another, muscles flowing like silk.

Sophia made the only logical choice. She fled.

CHAPTER 14

BURNE

B URNE WAS UNAWARE OF time as it dragged on in the dusty storage room. The latch of a trunk pressed into his spine, uncomfortable enough to keep him anchored. Fingernails traced patterns on his wool pants, an exercise his father had taught him when Burne was first learning to become a dragon. A man with a monster as large and lethal as a dragon living inside of him needed to maintain absolute control over his behavior lest he shift and cave the ceiling in.

Or shift and chase after his mate.

Why was it so tempting when she ran? He felt the way a cat must when they saw a mouse try to scurry out of harm's way.

Are you hunting me? Yes, the dragon absolutely was. The beast found the notion romantic. Never mind how terrifying it would be for a woman to turn back and find a dragon chasing her. What if he crushed her by mistake? Perhaps Sophia was right.

Stupid lizard. His dragon only scoffed, knowing he wouldn't crush her. He was nothing if not agile. He would treat his mate with the utmost care when he played with her.

"No playing with Sophia." Burne ordered aloud, as if that would sway his bestial half.

If he was being perfectly honest with himself, it wasn't merely the dragon who struggled to stay in place. Sophia was running from him, but it wasn't because he scared her. At least, not in the way that provoked terror. She *desired* him. It was plain in the flush of her cheeks, the erratic beat of her heart, the delicious smell of her—summer violets.

How could she not desire him? They were destined to become one in soul and flesh. Their attraction was inborn. Though, when he put it like that, Burne was a bit put off. He wanted Sophia to desire him because she saw him, not because of some divine force that selected a mate for him.

It was a silly system, really. What if they were incompatible? By all accounts, they should be. Sophia was the granddaughter of his worst enemy. Perhaps the Gods chose wrong. Or perhaps it was the dragon.

Pain lanced through his chest and along his spine, the dragon thrashing to take his skin. Apparently, the creature disagreed with Burne. Well, Burne disagreed with himself too. Prickly as she may be, he was already fond of the princess. Not only for her beauty—angelic as it was—but because she was bold. A queen should never be afraid to speak her mind to her king.

And that was what she would be. *His queen.* Even if it was only queen of a lonely, cavernous castle in the mountainside.

Now that his initial urge to pursue her had eased, Burne decided it safe to venture back out into the hall. The hour was growing late and Sophia was probably tired. She may even be asleep by the time he reached her door.

Asleep in my bed. Gods! He needed to think of something else. How did the day start with such a vicious fight but end with such a vicious hunger?

Food! Yes! That would be an excellent way to distract himself. Sate a different hunger. Only, the dining hall wouldn't serve him without Sophia's presence. What a ridiculous, awful spell. How was a man to get a midnight morsel if he had to drag his mate out of bed to do it?

Make her the midnight morsel instead. His dragon chimed in unhelpfully.

"Why did no one warn me that finding a mate was akin to going mad?" He muttered to himself, bare feet slapping loudly on the stone floor.

Burne followed the faint scent of Sophia directly to his chamber door. Was it wrong to be pleased that she hadn't moved rooms? At the very least, his bed would smell of her when she was gone.

What was he going to do to ensure she would never be gone?

Perhaps he should have bargained for more time. A fortnight? Or a month? He'd been so eager to get her to stay at any cost, he hadn't thought it through. He hadn't been at his most charming as of late. Hard to woo a woman when he was also dead set on revealing her family's sins to her. In hindsight, it would have made more sense to do it the other way around. First charm her and win her heart, *then* reveal that her grandfather was a murderous usurper.

Or Burne was cursed in some way and this courtship was doomed before it ever started. There was a chasm of family history between them, gaping and painful. How was he to build a bridge across it without succumbing to that pain?

By recognizing that Sophia was not guilty of her family's crimes, for one. No wonder she'd been so defensive. Damn him! How slow was he that it took two of his three days to grasp this?

The wood of the door was cool beneath his forehead. He hadn't noticed that he'd been leaning against it, breathing her in. Something was bothering him though, something the dragon was more keenly aware of than he.

There was no sound coming from inside. Understandable if she were asleep, except that he should at least hear her heartbeat. Her breath. Some sign of life. Burne stilled, listening as intently as he could.

There was no rustle of sheets, no feet scuffling on stone, no crackling of a fire in the hearth.

Sophia wasn't here.

Alarm surged to life inside of him. Had she tried to run away from him? It was a difficult climb but there was an exit suited for humans. It was for emergencies, a last resort if an enemy breached their defenses or a disaster left a dragon unable to leave with his family. It was also incredibly hidden. How would she even find it?

Well, he had left her unattended for most of the day.

Burne took off at a sprint, flying down the hallway so fast his heels broke off a chunk of stone. He whipped through the doorway to the dining hall, breathless and frantic, to find Sophia seated on the bench with a goblet in her hand. Startled, she dropped it, red liquid spilling over the side and pooling ominously on the table.

"Are you alright?" She asked, clutching her heart. "You look like you're being chased by a dragon." Warmth returned to her eyes as she laughed at her own humor.

He didn't know what to say to that. Her laughter caught him off guard, making him smile foolishly. What an oaf he was, winded and beaming at her like a lovesick puppy. Sophia must have thought so too. She shook her head, laughing again. Her amusement waned when she returned back to her goblet and remembered it was toppled.

"Can I conjure a napkin? Or will fairies come clean this up while I sleep?"

"I should hope there are no fairies in my home."

"You're right." She pointed to her chest. "I can cause enough mischief on my own."

"Is that what you're up to in here?" He feigned nonchalance, adrenaline still making his heart jolt.

"You're trying to distract me and it won't work. Why are you running through the halls in the middle of the night?" She glanced around the room. "It *is* night, isn't it? I feel a little mad not being able to look out the window."

"It is night." He agreed. "There's a balcony. I can show you in the morning when the sun comes up."

"Burne." She tsked. "You are a master of avoidance. Did you get a touch too excited and accidentally set your room on fire?" Sophia laughed again, puckering her lips to mime blowing fire.

"Exercise." He blurted stupidly. "I felt cooped up and needed some exercise."

"Are all dragons so ridiculous?"

"No. I'm one of a kind."

Sophia rolled her eyes heavenward, bringing them back down to look sadly at her spilled wine. "What a shame."

"Sorry."

"It's probably for the better. I don't actually like wine. I hoped it might help me sleep. Or at least warm me up." She rubbed up and down her arms. In her haste she'd chosen a dress that was obviously intended for somewhere warmer than the mountains. The sleeves were thin and scarcely covered her shoulders. The neckline dipped low enough between her breasts that it was almost scandalous.

Burne swallowed, forcing himself to focus on her goosebumps and not the delicious cream color of her exposed skin. "I can help you sleep. And warm you up."

Narrow blue eyes judged him warily. "Can you?"

Gods, he wished he was offering what it sounded like he was offering.

"It's my great grandmother's secret recipe. Mother used to drink it all winter long."

"How am I to summon a secret recipe I've never heard of?" She looked helplessly between him and the table.

"No need. Come with me." Burne didn't feel any less like a bouncing puppy as he led Sophia back down the hall, pulling open the door to the sitting room.

He could understand her complaint about windows. During the day the light was dull and filtered through the crystals that decorated the caverns. At night, the darkness in the chambers was fathomless without fire. His eyes adjusted quickly, picking up the faintest hints of starlight that gleamed through translucent pieces of crystal.

This room was his favorite place as a child, his sanctuary. His first action upon waking from his slumber was to uncover every plush chair and luxurious couch, flopping onto each one the way he had as a boy. He'd taken great care to restock the woodpile as well, stacking dozens of logs by the hearth. Three of them were ablaze in the fireplace within moments, filling the space with their dancing light.

"How do you keep from freezing to death during the colder months?" Sophia asked, hands outstretched to the fire. She was visibly trembling.

"Is it that cold in here?" He hadn't noticed. Fire ran through his blood, heating him in even the coldest settings. That didn't mean he *enjoyed* winter. Burne favored summer over any other season, but he could handle all of them better than a human. "When I was a boy there was a fire going in every room. My mother used to get cold too. She wore a pair of shoes made of bear fur every day, even in the summer."

"She hasn't left them lying around, has she?" Sophia joked, pointing one foot to the fire, then the other.

"I'm sorry, it's another thing I hadn't considered." All he had considered was keeping her. If he'd known the cost would be to her comfort, perhaps he would have reconsidered.

Nope. His dragon disagreed. *Keep her warm, oaf.*

"Stupid lizard." He hissed under his breath.

"Did you say something?"

"No. Sit down. I'll fetch you a blanket and a better drink than wine."

A minute later Burne had a wool blanket draped around her shoulders, another laid across her lap. The bottle in his hand was unopened, one of the very last left by his mother. Grief ran ghostly fingers over his heart, reminding him that there would be many *lasts* left by his parents. He knew his great grandmother's recipe was written somewhere in one of the many journals in the library but even if he made his own, it wouldn't be the same as being gifted it from his mother.

Sharing it with Sophia felt significant. She might not realize it but he was letting her in on an intimate family tradition. Many winter nights were spent curled in front of this fireplace, sipping heady drinks and entertaining each other with fairytales. The stories were best when his grandparents came for a stay. No one told a story like Ruby.

"If this doesn't warm you up, nothing will." Burne popped the cork, procuring two goblets from a table in the corner and pouring a healthy serving in each of them.

Sophia accepted the offered glass, sniffing it suspiciously. Reassured after watching him, she brought the drink to her lips and swallowed. "Gods!" Her eyes began to water. "What is this swill?"

He snorted so hard his drink nearly came out of his nostrils. "My grandmother called it 'Dragon's Breath.'"

"Aptly named." She coughed. "I don't think I can drink this.""Give it another try. I hated it my first time, too."

She obeyed, her nose wrinkling. "What is it, exactly?"

"It's a honey wine brewed with hot peppers and garlic"

"Hot peppers and garlic? Who makes wine with *garlic*?"

He raised his shoulders and dropped them back down, settling in a plush chair beside her. "My great grandmother. It used to be brewed as medicine. Ruby swore it could cure anything from a simple fever to an infection of the lungs."

Sophia paused with her goblet halfway to her mouth. "Ruby? You knew her?" "Of course, I did. She was my grandmother."

"But—how old are you?" She asked. "My grandfather wasn't a particularly young man when he took a wife, nor was my father. If you were old enough to remember your grandmother, you'd have to be half a century old." She studied his face. "It's not possible."

"I was eleven when Ruby died. She wasn't a particularly young woman either."

"You're lying." The accusation was instant. "There's no way you're nearly fifty."

"Dragons age at a different pace than humans. Haven't you heard the stories of dragons that lived five hundred years? Longer? When I reached maturity, my aging slowed dramatically." He sipped thoughtfully. "Though, I have also been asleep for nearly three decades."

"Ha!" Sophia scoffed. "Have you told me anything true?"

"I've yet to tell you a lie, princess."

They drank in silence for a time, her scrutinizing gaze never leaving him. When Burne refilled his goblet, he offered to do the same for her. She accepted, seeming to enjoy the unusual beverage more with every taste.

Finally, she demanded. "Explain it to me."

And so Burne did. He told her about dragon slumber, a type of hibernation that could stretch on for centuries. Most often a dragon went into slumber while he waited for his mate. Otherwise the loneliness and anticipation might drive him mad. That was the struggle with mating humans. The right woman might not come along for a hundred years.

When she did, some dragons were a little aggressive with their pursuit.

"I think that's where most myths about dragons stealing maidens come from." Burne told her. "Imagine waiting three hundred years for a bride. You might be a bit too enthusiastic when you discovered her."

"How does he know when to wake up?"

"How does a man turn into a dragon?" He shrugged. "Magic."

"Did you wake up on purpose then or do you have a mate out there waiting for you?" Was that a hint of disappointment in her tone?

"I have no mate out there." *She's right here beside me.* He'd made plenty of mistakes since meeting her two days ago. He wasn't going to make it worse by dropping that on her now. "But my waking was rather abrupt."

Waking from too many *hours* of sleep in the same position was uncomfortable. Waking from several decades of slumber with barely a movement was excruciating. Burne woke in the depths of the mountain, tucked safely in a cavern intended for exactly that. Even the faintest hint of sunlight through the crystals decorating the ceiling had been blinding to his long unused eyes.

The hunger forming a gnawing pit in his stomach was nearly unbearable too. Without use of the dining hall he was forced to the skies, ravenous and desperate for prey. He could understand how it might have been frightening for the people of Calos when he swooped down from the mountains, snatching sheep and cattle without prudence. In the time of his grandfather's reign, that would have been expected. The king compensated farmers generously for missing animals in their flocks.

It would have been a wiser choice for him to hunt in the lush forests at the base of the mountain. There were deer, elk, moose, many other small creatures that could sate his hunger in large enough numbers. The body of a dragon could be cumbersome though and navigating between trees on foot was neither graceful nor successful most of the time. Farm animals were easy pickings.

And once, long ago, hunting within the territory of the kingdom was necessary. His grandfather rarely left Calos and when he did, it was never by flight. The dragon was revered as a protector. Losing livestock to him was considered a blessing. Shepherds bolstered their flocks in expectation of the sacrifice, to honor the beast that roamed their night skies, guarding the kingdom from enemies.

What sort of world would they live in if that were still the case? Burne had slept so long. He hadn't a clue what shape life had taken outside these stone walls. Sophia made it sound better than before, less brutal now that *her* grandfather was gone. But could the seed of the fruit grow a different tree? Or was he doomed to want a woman who would be his downfall?

Burne drew back into focus, realizing that Sophia had fallen silent, studying him. She drained her cup, a rosy tint flooding her cheeks. The blanket around her shoulders was beginning to slide, baring only one pale arm. Gods, she really was beautiful. Bathed in shimmering firelight, her dark hair damp and tousled, her eyes hazy with drink but still as deeply blue as the sky, she was breathtaking.

How many had seen her like this? None, Burne prayed. He desperately wanted this image to be his alone. Always. The sharp-tongued princess was not easily made vulnerable, not often exposed, and he was pleased to be allowed to delve behind her walls, even if it was slightly coerced.

"Why were you asleep to begin with? Didn't you have responsibilities? Desires?" She held out her cup, allowing him to pour her more. It wasn't his intention to intoxicate her, but who was he to stop her if she wanted to continue? Sophia was safe to drop as many inhibitions as she liked here. Burne would never take advantage.

"My responsibilities were to my mate, my family, and my kingdom. I had none of those when I became a man. I was alone. So, I waited. What more could I do? I was hardly going to storm your family's castle and murder your father."

"Perhaps you should have." Sophia mused. "You would get your throne back and I would get my freedom."

"What makes you think I would set you free? Maybe I would have made you my queen."

"Ha! And forsake the mystical woman the Gods have divined for you?"

Burne mulled his drink with his tongue, crafting a careful response. "I would never forsake her."

Sophia hid her crestfallen expression in her goblet, gulping down the rest of her wine. So she did feel it too. She wouldn't understand it, perhaps didn't even want it, but the call was as present for her as it was for him. The difference was that she didn't have an eager dragon whispering encouragement in her mind.

"I should consider myself lucky." She said blithely. "The only one trying to force a match on me is my father. Your match was chosen for you by the Gods. They are much more capricious than the King of Calos."

"Indeed, they are." Mischievous or cruel, Burne hadn't decided yet. He supposed the decision would be dependent on the outcome of his time with her.

"You speak fondly of your parents but you claim to have no family. What happened to them?"

"Is there a subject that you find inappropriate to prod at? Or do you interrogate everyone you meet?" He posed the question without heat, finding her boldness more and more endearing.

She waggled her cup at him. "If you didn't wish for me to interrogate you, then you shouldn't have loosened an already audacious tongue."

"Fair enough." Burne slid from his recliner, leaning his elbows on his knees as he settled beside the hearth. The flames danced their heated dance over the logs, a contrast to the dark, damp grief that hung over memories of his parents. He pressed the rim of his goblet to his chin, eyes growing out of focus as he recalled the last time he saw them.

"My mother was often ill. It is the reason I have no brothers or sisters, at least none that lived." He swallowed back the fresh pain at the memory of his mother silently crying when she thought he wasn't watching, mourning another baby that came too soon. "She was always joking that she would catch her death in this mountain home. She hated the cold. Sometimes I wonder if the Gods heard her and thought it amusing to play a cruel joke of their own."

Sophia surprised him by joining him on the plush fur rug, her hand resting sympathetically on his arm. If anyone could understand the particular heartbreak of losing a mother, it was her. Burne had been fortunate to have a long and happy childhood with her before she began deteriorating.

"She was feverish and bedridden for nearly a year before she succumbed to whatever ailed her. My father tried all manner of treatments for her—brought her to medicine women, even found a doctor in a kingdom far to the east—with no success. Most days he spent by her bedside. They both withered away, her because of sickness and him because his heart was dying."

"I'm sorry." Her fingers squeezed him gently, sending tingles up his arm through his clothing. She removed her hand swiftly, eyeing it suspiciously and flexing. Did that mean she felt it too? Imagine the sensation if she allowed him to explore her unrestricted.

The quiet condolence soothed him. Often he found those words empty, the pleasantries required to end the uncomfortable conversation. Sophia never said anything that she didn't mean. For all that it could be vexing, he admired that about her.

Curiosity fluttered in her eyes as they shot him sidelong glances. There was more that she wanted to ask, another question lingering in her throat that, for once, she felt was better left unspoken. Burne decided to reward her politeness by sating that curiosity.

"You're wondering how my father died if dragons live such long lives." Sophia looked up at him, surprised, and nodded. "We are usually quite difficult to kill. Unless, of course, we're mated."

That was another pitfall of taking a human mate. When a bond was made between dragon and woman, the dragon's life was quite literally bound to his mate. He would grow weak and ill upon her death, his excessive years catching up to him within days, sometimes hours. Father held out three days before he passed, still cradling the body of his mate in his arms.

Perhaps it wasn't a disadvantage to taking a human mate after all. What man would want to outlive his wife and potential daughters by centuries?

"Is a bond like a marriage contract?" Sophia wondered, breaking him from his dark thoughts.

"A marriage contract is exactly that. A contract. An agreement between two parties, usually with mutual benefit. A bond is a choice, a connection ordained by the Gods that locks two souls together. Marriage is little more than a trade arrangement compared to the bond a dragon will share with his mate."

"Your tone makes it sound romantic, but I'm not entirely sure the idea of *locking one's soul to another* is pleasant. Does it make you a prisoner? What if you change your mind? Can you break the bond?"

"A bond is only broken by death." He explained, holding her gaze seriously. "If you made that choice, you would never change your mind. Not when you are tied so thoroughly and completely to your mate. Their heart beats in time with yours, their every emotion open to you."

"And how do you make this bond?"

Burne grinned wickedly, tracing the lines of her body from toes to nape with his eyes. "The same way you consummate a marriage."

"What if you bond with the wrong woman?"

"How could you bond with the wrong woman?"

"The same way a man puts a baby in a woman who isn't his wife."

Something dangerous came to life inside him as he began to wonder how much experience and knowledge Sophia had on such matters. Had she taken lovers before him?

"You wait for your mate. It is expected that your mate waits for you too."

She chortled. "So, dragons are centuries old virgins. No wonder they snatch maidens up so fervently."

Before Burne could dig any deeper into the subject, Sophia changed it, easily firing off another question about his kind. That was probably for the better. What tactful way was there for him to inquire about her history and any man she may have been...well acquainted with? Burne had little justification for such intrusive conversation.

"Tell me a story about being a dragon." She requested, reclining comfortably on the rug, fingers lazily drawing patterns in the fur.

"Whatever the princess wants." He smiled at her, beginning a story of the first time he learned to fly.

Amusement glittered in her eyes like the luminescent lights in the bathing pool. Burne scratched his chin, delving into his memory to find more lighthearted stories to draw out her laughter. Sophia didn't have a delicate, ladylike laugh. Her joy was raucous and contagious, filling a space within him that had been empty until her unexpected arrival.

They were at least four drinks in when her laughter devolved into snorting fits. Burne felt the hum of alcohol in his veins, but it was evident that he'd spent much more time in his cups than Sophia. She carelessly flopped back onto the floor, her arm draped over his lap.

The contact was so distracting that he didn't immediately understand what she requested next. When he did, Burne had to shimmy his hips away from her, lest she feel the way her words sent blood pumping between his thighs.

"What?" He shook his head, sure he'd misunderstood her in his haze of lust.

"May I touch him?" Sophia's eyes flicked over his form, her eagerness indistinguishable from arousal.

"Him?" Burne dipped his chin to glance between his legs then back at her.

"Your *dragon!*"

The creature burst to life, scales pressing against his skin. Burne had to chug the rest of his drink and grit his teeth to keep from shifting right then and there.

You said you wouldn't crush her. He reminded his inner beast. The dragon was prancing around like a playful puppy, angry with Burne for holding back. It was his turn to spend time with Sophia. She wanted him.

His mind conjured an image of her touching his other *dragon,* making him rise from the floor a little too urgently and adjust his pants. "Dragon." He muttered stupidly.

"Or was it all a trick and I only dreamt you shifted from dragon to man?"

He tugged her up from the floor, practically trotting to the door. "You should be more careful about teasing a dragon, princess."

She rushed to keep up with him, grabbing the crook of his elbow with her spare hand. "A queen does as she pleases."

His eyes were fully shifted when he turned to look back at her. Her form shimmered, delicious waves of heat emanating from her bare skin. "Yes, she certainly does."

Sophia questioned their journey half a hundred times before they reached their destination. The cavernous ceilings in most of the chambers were taller than ordinary rooms but none were fit to accommodate a dragon. If she wished to see him changed it would have to be in the entryway. Stone columns held up the arched ceiling, making the perfect runway between them.

Years of practice made it possible for Burne to fly in and out of the narrow tunnel with ease. That wasn't always the case. As a young dragon he'd been clumsy, his body ungainly and his wings foreign even after dozens of flights. There were many days where he flew in after his father, legs tucked too tight, turning his body into a projectile with far too much momentum. More than one of the stone pillars had come dangerously close to collapsing when he rammed into it horns first.

"You may want to avert your eyes." He warned.

"But I want to see!"

His shirt flew from his chest, landing at her feet. Hands hovered at the top of his trousers, ready to part with them too. "What do you want to see, Sophia?" The growl reverberating in his throat made the question sound like a purr.

She sputtered, finally echoing his mindless utterance from moments earlier. "Dragon."

"I'll show you my dragon." Burne hesitated, letting her drink in his bare form.

And drink she did. Sophia's teeth pinched her plush bottom lip, eyes shamelessly wandering over every inch of him. If the expression of want on her face wasn't enough to test his self-control, the delicious violet scent of her permeating the space between them was.

He stepped back, opening the link between himself and the dragon before he did something rash like take her in his arms and kiss her. At this point she probably wouldn't protest, but Burne wouldn't take advantage of her intoxication.

Scales spread over his skin first. Then came the claws and horns, pushing from the tips of his fingers and breaking through his skull. Burne hunched forward, his spine lengthening, limbs thickening, shoulders opening up to allow for his broad wingspan. The transformation should have been horrifying, a grotesque display of pain as his body was remade.

And maybe it was unsettling to witness, if Sophia fainting the first time was any way to judge. It was never painful, though. Scorching heat engulfed him, but it was a heat he was accustomed to, a heat he longed for, a burning that made him feel alive. A proud roar formed in his diaphragm, shaking the cavern around them. Leathery, gold wings stretched in a showy display for her, buffeting her hair as they stretched.

"Gods," Sophia muttered, backpedaling until she bumped into the nearest stone pillar.

Burne eyed her, craned his head to hear her heartbeat, tasting her scent for any sign of fear. It was easy for him to tell her that he wouldn't hurt her in this form, but difficult for her to trust that. Especially when she was face to face with a head the size of a horse.

She didn't appear frightened but she wasn't coming any closer either. The request had been to *touch* him, something his dragon would not easily forget. He decided to try a different tactic, tucking his wings and lowering to his belly. He dropped his head to the ground, gaze even with her.

"I'll give you horrible indigestion if you eat me." Said Sophia, the faintest quaver in her voice. "I've been told I'm quite sour."

Burne snorted and she jumped. It took her several bated breaths to recognize it was a noise of amusement. When she did, she smiled back at him, stepping closer still.

"I've never seen a lizard with horns." She mused, eyeing the curled fixtures that jutted out of his skull.

He lifted his head, pressing his nose into her and knocking her sideways. A dragon was *not* a lizard. Instead of losing her nerve, as he feared she would, Sophia threw her head back with a wild laugh. "You don't like being called a lizard either? Very well. I surrender." *I knew you would eventually.* "Now behave yourself, dragon. I've seen your teeth. I don't want to know the feel of them."

Feeling playful, he lifted his lip as if to say, "these teeth?" Her eyes widened as she reached out, fingers coming out to grip an incisor. She squealed and jumped backwards when his tongue darted out to lick her arm.

"I haven't given you permission to kiss me, dragon." Sophia chided, dancing to the side so she could get a better look at his snout.

Ordinarily a dragon wasn't a particularly polite creature but he held himself back from tasting her again. The victory would be even sweeter when he was given permission. Sooner or later she would cave to her desire. That was how this worked, wasn't it?

Scales rasped against her skin as she smoothed her palm over his face, tracing the curve of his jaw until she came to its end. From there she lifted onto the tips of her toes, straining to reach a curled horn. Burne shifted his head, pressing his face against her stomach under the guise of giving her better access.

The scent of her was even more delicious in this form, if that was possible. Violets and summer rain mingled with a hint of pungent spice. Her mouth would taste like garlic if he kissed her now. He wouldn't mind so long as she was giving herself to him.

Sophia's exploration continued all the way to the tip of his tail. She paused halfway between tail and head, craning her neck to study his wings. "May I touch them too?"

Burne stretched out his wing, lowering it over her so that she could easily reach. A satisfied rumble vibrated in his belly when her gentle fingers made contact with the leathery skin. No one had ever touched his wings before. He hadn't realized how sensitive they were, how much it would make his blood pump to have her hands tracing the veiny structures.

"They appear to be so fragile," She said, more to herself than him. "But they feel so sturdy." The smile she flashed him was drunken and amused. "What is that noise? Are you *purring*?"

Close enough. Her touch was turning him into a useless, tame creature. And she wasn't stopping any time soon. Burne relaxed onto his side as she learned every scaled detail, marveling at claws and horns, verbally admiring the color of him.

She lost her energy before she lost her interest, leaning against his face with a noisy yawn. The honey wine must have impacted her even more than he suspected. Moments later she was plopping down onto the floor, curling around his leg and resting her head on his clawed foot.

"You are *so* warm. I wish I could use you as a blanket."

You certainly could.

Burne carefully extricated himself from her hold, shifting back and dressing quickly. He hoisted a bleary Sophia from the floor, leading her back to the sitting room and lowering her onto the couch. Perhaps he should send her to bed.

Not yet, he begged no one in particular. Loneliness was his only friend for decades and now it was chased away by a beauty with a viper's tongue. Burne would cling to this night until the sun rose, if he had to.

"Tell me more dragon stories." Sophia murmured, seeming equally attached to their finite time together.

Burne obliged, talking until long after her breathing was even and her eyelids were sealed for the night. With any luck, the sound of his voice would carry into her dreams and keep him locked firmly in her mind. It may be the only way to burrow into that safeguarded heart of hers.

CHAPTER 15

SOPHIA

S OPHIA'S EYELIDS FLUTTERED LAZILY. Her body felt warm and pliable. The faintest hint of garlic lingered on her tongue—Gods her breath must be terrible—but there was none of the discomfort she'd been told to expect from overindulging in wine or spirits. Despite being sprawled on the couch in Burne's sitting room, she slept quite comfortably.

She glanced over the edge of the cushion to see Burne curled on the rug below her, their fingers meeting. Apparently, she wasn't the only one who slept comfortably.

He was rather breathtaking. The last of the firelight made his dark blonde locks shimmer. His skin looked to be gilded and firm, just a touch thicker than an ordinary man. Though his features had an easy charm to them, he wasn't *pretty* like her brother George or some of the young lords of the court. Burne was statuesque, every part of him angled and hard.

On their own volition her eyes wandered lower, staring between his legs and remembering that it truly was *all* of him when he shed his clothes the night before. Sophia knew it *could* do that but she'd never actually seen it. Why did she want to see it again?

Burne shifted onto his back and Sophia came to realize that her observations were not strictly made by her gaze. She quickly yanked her hand away from where she was *petting* him. What was it about this man that made her feel so out of control? Did he have her under some sort of spell? Ordinarily Sophia was immune to even the most beguiling men, seeing through their mask.

And Gods, she'd never thought herself wanton before, but the man had her twisted six ways.

"You can't keep your hands off me." A bleary smile decorated Burne's face. His sleep laden voice was gravely in a way that made goosebumps dot her arms.

Sophia scoffed. "Intoxicated affection is not true affection."

"Do I intoxicate you, princess? Because you've spent your morning caressing me and unless you've broken into another bottle, you should be sober."

She huffed, coming to a seated position and crossing her arms.

"Stubborn." Burne tutted, gripping her chin between thumb and pointer finger. When Sophia didn't move away, he brushed his thumb along her bottom lip. "I've woken from many nights of drinking and never seen a view this beautiful."

"Oh?" A sudden pang of jealousy sprung up. "So, I'm the prettiest woman you've woken to find beside you after a night in your cups?"

The grin that stretched his lips was devastating, a predator that knew he'd cornered his prey. "Certainly."

His hand dropped from her face. Sophia watched him arch his spine, stretching languidly until the muscles in his back became visible through the taut fabric of his shirt. How many other women touched those muscles, fingers digging in as they shared a moment of ecstasy? The image played on repeat in her head, growing more detailed the more she tried to ignore it.

"Do you make a habit of this? Kidnapping women, forcing them to spend time with you, then seducing them once you've convinced them to overindulge in drink?"

He laughed—*laughed*—at her biting words. "Would it make you jealous if I did?"

"It would make you another uninspiring man who thinks with the tool between his legs." Sophia stood, stomping from the couch to the hearth. She wrenched the fire poker out of the stand like a weapon, stabbing aggressively at the ashes. Burne was lucky he wasn't receiving the brunt of her anger. She stabbed again, harder.

What. Was. Wrong. With. Her?

Burne kidnapped her. He was a stupid lizard man who held her captive because of some twisted revenge plot against her family. So long as he kept his word and brought her home, he didn't matter. And yet, Sophia felt as if she'd eaten a dozen live fish when she thought of him laying with other women.

She'd scarcely even touched him herself.

Burne's expression shifted, eyes growing golden as his tone became deadly seriously. "I would never forsake my mate, no matter how long and lonely the nights are."

The words splashed over her like an icy wave, drowning the heat of jealousy and anger, leaving a painful emptiness in their wake. Good. Sophia had desperately needed that reminder of reality.

"Your three days are up, lizard." She said coolly.

"The third day has only begun."

"I don't care." She snapped. "It's time."

"Uh-uh, princess. Don't go back on your word."

Sophia turned, poker still in hand. "Or what?"

"Ah, you've caught me in your trap. I'm not a captor and I will not keep you against your will." He wrapped fingers around her hand and gently removed her makeshift weapon. "If I deliver you in broad daylight, there is a greater risk to your safety. It's endearing that the archers on the wall think their puny arrows can harm a dragon but less so when I think of those arrows accidentally hitting you."

Sophia's hand tingled where he touched her. "How very clever of you."

"Not cleverness." He rested the poker back on the stand. "I'm merely being logical."

Heat engulfed her, somehow greater than that of the fire. Sophia whirled on her heel, nearly smacking into his chest. Gold swirled over umber, trapping her gaze in the pools of dancing color. Smoke and spice wafted from him the way a warm cookie let off scent. She was suddenly overcome with a terrible and inexplicable sadness. She was going to miss the scent of dragon. And the freedom she gained when she was with him.

She could call him captor all day, but in truth, Burne had liberated her. Here there were no marriage contracts, no arrogant kings or spoiled brothers, no lords and ladies with upturned noses. Here, nothing was expected of her.

It was her duty to return to Calos, to do what she could to share that same liberation with her people, but it was a relief to take a rest from it all.

Sparks climbed up her neck when Burne gently cupped it. "Why do you look so sad, Sophia?"

The answer sat on the edge of her tongue. It took three tries to swallow it but she managed to bite back the honesty and instead answered, "I fear what I will return to in Calos."

The gold became dominant in his eyes, a bright glow around pin-prick irises. "I won't return you if your safety is not guaranteed."

"I'm not worried for myself." Though her safety *wasn't* guaranteed now that her petulant brother had his right to the throne questioned by his subjects. "I worry for the people who stood against my father.

What if he discovered their identities? I may have to release them all from the dungeon."

"You will make right all that your father has done wrong."

She blew out a breath, vulnerability chipping away at her hardened veneer. "How?"

"You're a bright woman, Sophia. You'll know what to do when the time comes." Sophia raised her hand, resting it over his heart. The organ thumped wildly, as if it sought her affection through his ribs. "Or you could stay."

"What?"

"You could stay here with me and never have to face what troubles you." Burne's voice was a deep vibration, a purr that lulled her into a false security.

"Don't." She shoved him away, moving until the couch was between them. "Don't toy with me."

"I mean what I've said."

"Stay here and do what? Read through every book in your library? Swim around in your magic pool and drink away every evening? Feast on all the richest foods until I'm a gluttonous size?"

"Yes, that sounds fantastic."

Fairytales usually did.

"I could be the queen of a giant cave."

"Yes." Burne laughed. "Queen Sophia of the dragon cave."

Was he really this cruel? Or simply stupid?

"Until you find that woman you're so enamored with." Sophia would not let him see the dejected look that tried to take her face. She would not show him weakness.

"No—"

"I'm hungry." She interrupted, hurrying to the dining hall before he could play any more games with her wayward heart.

The man was self-centered and out of touch. The man wasn't a *man* at all. Clearly, he and his beast were at odds. The dragon wanted one person and that person was not she.

And perhaps, she thought bitterly, Burne didn't want *her* at all. Perhaps he was a smooth liar and that mysterious woman meant nothing to him. Sophia was a warm body. That was enough for most men.

Her captivity was clearly intended to get some kind of leverage over her father—leverage Burne quickly discovered he wouldn't gain—and any amicability between them was merely a convenience that offered him female companionship.

Doubt niggled and wormed through her sour thoughts, but she squashed it down, focusing on making it to the dining table without her emotions overcoming her.

"Sophia!"

"Will you starve when I'm gone?" She asked cheerily, fixing him with her courteous princess smile. "Or do you plan to kidnap another woman to make your magic table work?"

"I haven't kidnapped you." He growled, the sound bouncing around the open chamber.

"We shall agree to disagree."

Burne gripped her upper arm. "Sophia, please—"

"You have two more meals with me. Make them count." She jerked out of his hold. "What would you like to eat? Dream up anything and I will make it yours."

Damn him and those heated looks. Sophia averted her eyes and began thinking of all the desserts she planned to break her fast with. This was her last chance to eat anything she could dream of and she was going to take advantage.

Burne was wise enough to drop his pleas as they ate, instead choosing to entertain her with more stories of learning to be a winged creature after a lifetime as a boy. They gorged themselves—her on pastries and him on tender meats—and laughed well past morning. Sophia's rear was sore from staying seated on a wooden bench for hours but she was enjoying herself too much to move.

Burne was a pleasant companion. His sense of humor matched hers, sardonic with a touch of darkness. The jokes he told were the kind that drew laughter deep from her belly, the kind Rosemary would gasp at and deem wicked.

They'd scarcely finished eating before Burne was hungry for lunch. Sophia couldn't bear the thought of another bite, but she gladly called up whatever foods he desired. They turned it into a game, her thinking up the oddest dishes she'd tried and him judging the taste. He wasn't keen on pickled eggs or the wet eggplant dish from some southern island near Gazar, but he enjoyed the crispy buns filled with pork and ginger.

Perhaps when all of this was done, they could remain friends. Sophia didn't know how it would be possible, but she wanted to try. When he wasn't badgering her with family history and she wasn't sniping at him to keep her guard up, they found a rather enjoyable peace.

"What was it like? Living here when you were a child?"

The question was a welcome distraction for both of them as the day ticked by and their departing hour neared. Burne delved into tale after tale of his upbringing, the trouble he got into, his mother's constant frustration with his inability to sit still.

"Raising a dragon," he explained, "is not as simple as raising a boy."

Sophia laughed when he told her of how he *did* accidentally set his bedchamber on fire. More than once. Whatever ancestor chose to make their family home inside stone walls had been very wise indeed.

It withstood fire and the many tussles between him and his father. A wooden hall would have crumbled to ashes centuries ago.

"It wasn't always easy to live here. I had very little contact with others my age." He drank deeply from his cup, enjoying more of the heady honey wine from the night before. "I longed for a little brother to race down the hallways and climb the stone pillars. Someone to share my secrets with."

"We have that in common, it seems."

Her comment must have rankled because he frowned, asking, "How could you be lonely in a castle surrounded by people? With a brother and a father? And your Rosemary?"

"A matronly handmaid, a rotten brother, and a controlling father do not make especially delightful friends."

"So, you pity yourself because you don't like your brother?"

"I do not *pity* myself." She ground out. "Have you crowned yourself king of loneliness? Sitting on his isolated throne in self-righteous glory?"

"Do you think *you* have suffered such a miserable life because you didn't get your way?" The sudden flare of his temper was startling. The heat of it spread, catching the incendiary mood that had been sitting like kindling beneath her skin. She felt strange and vulnerable, and she masked it with ire.

"Am I not allowed to have suffered simply because I was born a princess? Am I allowed no grief? No bitterness? No turmoil to call my own?"

"Perhaps not." He pushed back from the table, putting distance between them.

"You really are ill-tempered, aren't you?"

Burne turned back to her, expression tight. "You really are *spoiled*, aren't you?"

Somehow that word, that one silly word, thrown at her daily for countless years, became a sword in his hands, cutting into her heart and wounding her more gravely than a stranger should have been able to. Sophia didn't care if her father and George thought her spoiled. It bothered her little to know the lords and ladies believed she thought herself superior to them. Even the people of Calos were allowed to think her pampered. How could they not when they had so little knowledge of her?

But to hear that awful word from Burne felt cruel. Sophia had opened herself to him, sharing fragile places that no one else had touched. She foolishly thought he would be gentle with them, might even cherish them. Why would he? Sophia was nothing to him but the wretched seed of a usurper, a spoiled princess with no care for anyone but herself.

"I am *spoiled*," She began, her voice void of the hurt that tore at her insides. "Because it is my armor. I was not alone in a mountain with no children to befriend. I was alone in a castle full of them, spurned by my peers. My stone walls had windows and doors, but they imprisoned me no less." Her lip threatened to tremble, so she bit down on it hard enough to draw blood. "All of my life I was told that I was *hated*. My people despised me, the nobles of the court thought me too antagonistic and unladylike.

"I was so reviled that my father tried to pawn me off on fat merchants and wealthy mercenaries. So, I became *spoiled* to protect myself from a fate that would slowly destroy me. I am *spoiled,* Burne Baxenstone because I would rather be loathed for my tongue than capitulate to some disgusting man who wants little more than a broodmare. If I wanted to be dragged unwilling to the marriage bed of a man who thought it beneath him to offer me a modicum of respect, I would have perched pretty and polite at my father's side."

"Sophia, I didn't mean—"

"Your three days are over." She interrupted sharply. "Take me home."

Chapter 16

DUSK STRETCHED INDIGO WINGS on the horizon opposite Burne, painting the valley in pink and purple hues. The air was more frigid than when she was first spirited away but the view of the sunset over Calos was breathtaking. Sophia mourned her last chance to see the world from this spectacular height even as she enjoyed it.

The hole in her heart grew larger at the same pace as the kingdom until there was a castle of anguish inside of her just as there was a castle in the valley before her. Burne was careful to keep a distance from the walls when he brought them down, circling fields and sending flocks of sheep fleeing in terror. Eventually they landed close enough to the main gate for guards to see her coming on foot but far enough that the arrows they might loose couldn't hit her.

Though, Sophia wasn't sure why he was so cautious. The walls were remarkably quiet. No shouts called out the presence of the dragon, no whistling of arrows dotting the air. The entire kingdom seemed to have slipped indoors for an early slumber.

When she dismounted from Burne's clawed foot and approached the city wall, she began to feel an itch of uncertainty. The quiet was eerie, upsetting the hairs on her nape. Burne bowed his bestial head, golden eyes scanning the area warily. His nostrils flared, breath coming in and out of his massive lungs like a blacksmith bellow. She took several steps away from him, eyeing the wall suspiciously. Had they decorated for a holiday that she'd forgotten? There were strange shapes lining the parapets, accented here and there with barely visible flares of red.

"Sophia, wait!" Burne's voice came choked and urgent but she ignored him, not interested in being coerced.

"Goodbye, Burne."

His bare feet rustled the long grass as he ran after her, his urgency increasing with every step between them. "Don't, Sophia! Don't move."

Sophia stilled. Perhaps he saw an archer lining up a shot or some other danger that her eyes couldn't pick up in the darkening evening.

No. She told herself. *Don't let him pull you back in. Don't let your heart be weak.*

She only marched two more steps before she was frozen again, this time in horror at the realization of what—no, *who*—dangled from the front gate.

Red patches of fabric stained the arms of a dozen—no, two dozen—hanging bodies, the only color on their filthy, decaying forms save for the purple hues of their once pale faces. One lifeless face stood out among the corpses, even in her horrifying state. Rosemary swayed softly in the wind, her feet scuffling against the top of the gatehouse. That breeze shifted Sophia's way, bringing with it the putrid odor of carrion.

The scream that wrenched from her lungs seemed to echo through the whole valley, shaking the walls and bringing the earth up to meet her. Only when Burne's arms came around her did she realize it was the other way around and she had tumbled to the ground. Another keening wail left her throat raw. It was nothing compared to the pain beneath her ribs.

Rosemary, dear, sweet Rosemary. And so many other innocents, people who died for their cause. They were ready to die in her name.

Warm arms encircled her, holding her steady as she sobbed into the grass. As quickly as he was beside her, Burne was absent, leaving her cold and more alone than she'd ever felt. She felt the tingle of his presence behind her and heard the whoosh of wings just before they came around her like a shield.

That was when Sophia became aware of the shouting. An arrow whistled over the dragon's shoulder. Another sliced into the skin of Burne's wing. It didn't penetrate but it had to have hurt.

"Cease fire! That's the princess!" Someone shouted.

"That's a Gods-damned dragon! Kill it!"

A mighty roar trumpeted through the air, causing Sophia to stumble and lose her footing again. Burne snapped viciously, his maw pointed at the gate house. She couldn't see what was happening but she prayed he wouldn't set them ablaze. They were only trying to protect the kingdom, foolhardy as that may be.

More shouting intermixed with tremendous roars. The ground rumbled as if an earthquake was upon them. Sophia clung to Burne's clawed foot when he stretched it out to grasp her. She shrieked when they lifted into the air unexpectedly, icy wind nearly ripping the cloak from her shoulders. Her stomach dipped when Sophia glanced back to watch Calos rapidly disappearing behind them. They were flying much faster than the journey here. Twilight was quickly passing and seeing nothing but the vague shapes below—very far below—made her ill with terror

For the remainder of the flight, Sophia kept her eyes squeezed shut. She was dizzy and shaking violently when Burne gently set her on the stone floor of his entry hall. Sophia collapsed against the nearest pillar, hands covering her face.

Her cheek pressed into the naked skin of Burne's chest when he snaked his arms around her, pulling her into his lap. Instantly the chill receded from her body as his warmed her better than a blazing fire. Sparks crackled everywhere they met, bringing her frozen parts back to life. Sophia let him hold her as a torrent of tears wet her face. Gentle hands caressed her back, soothing each shuddering sob away.

"I'm so sorry, love."

Anger flared amidst her grief and she lurched backward. "This is your fault!" She shouted, shoving to her feet. "I should have been there. I could have protected them."

"No, sweet Sophia."

His soft tone only increased her aggravation. "Yes! I could have! I could have saved them." She insisted shrilly. "This is all your fault."

Sophia pummeled uselessly at his arms and chest when he came for her. Burne took her abuse, letting her fight his embrace until she'd clawed the last of her fury out. She slumped into him, defeated, and he scooped her up, cradling her carefully as he carried her through the dining hall and all the way to his chamber. He settled her onto the bed so delicately, as if she might shatter were he too rough.

Sophia was already shattering into a thousand painful pieces.

Burne was dressed when he sat on the edge of the bed to cup her hand. Fire roared in the hearth and she wondered how long she'd lain there listlessly. It was long enough to etch lines of concern into Burne's handsome features.

"You were right." She croaked. "My father is a monster and I'm poisoned by the blood of a violent tyrant."

"No, Sophia, I was wrong." He brought the backs of her fingers to his lips, holding them there. "I judged you for your heritage without remembering that even an apple at the base of the tree can grow a wild variation on the fruit it was made from."

"So I grow tart, unappealing apples instead of rotten ones?"

"There she is." He smiled briefly. "You grow fruit that could nourish an entire generation. Cold hardy, well kept, with a touch of sweetness."

"Why are you being kind to me?"

"Why wouldn't I be kind to you?"

"You hate me and my family. You think I'm nothing more than a spoiled princess."

Guilt deepened the lines on his face. "Sophia, please forgive me. I've done all of this so wrong." He rubbed his thumb up and down her knuckles. "I don't know why I was so intent on proving to you that your grandfather wronged my family. It would change nothing between us." He brought her hand back to his lips and kissed her lightly. "I was only seeing what I believed to be true about you. Not what my dragon wanted me to see."

Her heart hammered madly against her ribs. "And what was that?"

"That you're precisely what I need." He huffed out a nervous breath. "That I deserve the sharpest edge of your tongue. That I was meant for someone who could match my stubborn pride."

Perhaps it was the grief that weighed on her like a boulder, breaking her open into a vulnerable enough state to allow him in. Or perhaps her own inner beast, the wild and lonely creature that kept others at bay, recognized the same thing his dragon did. Burne made her furious, but he also made her feel alive. He thrilled her.

And whether or not he would admit it, they were the same. They lived the same lonely lives, wanted the same future for the kingdom that belonged to neither of them yet should belong to both of them.

But she never wanted *this*. Sophia dreaded the day her father finally found her a suitor that stuck. Her days would be wasted as a primped and pretty doll, her nights suffered through as some grunting man twice her age tried to get her with child.

Burne was not her father's choice though, was he? For a daring moment Sophia dreamed of what it would look like to choose for herself. She could spend her days reading, laughing, swimming in caves lit by enchanted starlight. At night she would be wrapped in smoke and sandalwood, wrapped in strong arms that held her for the sake of holding her. If she wanted him to, he would make love to her for the sake of making love, not heirs.

It felt a selfish, frivolous dream to stay in this isolated castle forever. In that moment, she wanted nothing more. She wanted to forget her grief and her terrible father. Sophia wanted to lose herself in something hopeful.

"Do you mean what I think you mean?"

"My dragon chose you the moment your scent caught the breeze. You called to me from miles away, your presence a throbbing awareness in my soul. I knew you were out there waiting for me, ready for me."

"Why didn't you tell me?" She whispered to the pillow, turning from him, too afraid to hope yet.

"I had my reasons, though they seem foolish now."

"Give them to me."

"Demanding princess." Burne chuckled. "At first, I was angry when I discovered who you were to me. I thought the Gods were playing a cruel trick. Then I behaved like a pompous ass, and I was too afraid to tell you. I didn't want you to think me another man who merely wanted to possess your beauty and your status."

"You don't think me beautiful? Wouldn't you want to be my king?" She couldn't hold her tongue even when she tried.

Burne gave her a flat look. "You're stunning—literally breathtaking—and you know it." Sophia blinked innocently as he continued. "And I would rule by your side even if we rule over nothing but stone."

"Say it plainly then. Who am I to you? What do you want from me?"

"You're my mate, Sophia." The golden glow swirled to life in his eyes. "And I want everything from you."

CHAPTER 17

BURNE

BURNE STARED AT HER, not daring to blink—not daring to breathe—until she spoke. Now was the wrong time to do this. She was grieving. But he'd already messed the whole situation up so royally and he was worried if he wasn't honest now, she might still want to go back to that death trap. Sophia felt obligated to her people—as any good queen should—and she would risk her life to protect those who tried to protect her. He wouldn't have that.

As much as Burne wanted to spread his wings and fly right back to Calos, burning away the murderous king and clearing the path for him and Sophia to rule, he wasn't sure it was the right decision. Another part of him couldn't bear the thought of putting her at risk. The scent of carrion still stung his nostrils and he couldn't stop picturing Sophia as one of those dangling bodies. Would her father go that far to ensure her brother made it to the throne?

"Mate?" She cut through his thoughts. "A wife that the Gods chose for you?"

"So much more than that." He lowered her palm to press it over his heart. "A soul designed to match mine in every way."

"Do I belong to you even if I am unwilling?"

The question pierced his insides, leaving his lungs deflated. "No." He choked out. "I offer you all of myself, but you have no obligation to take any part of me."

"We've only just met."

"We have a lifetime to become acquainted."

"What if I want to go back?" She slipped her hand from his, fidgeting with the corner of the blanket. "To Calos?"

His dragon roared a protest, remembering the sting of arrows that missed her only because of his wings. Burne denied the beast. Sophia would never agree to stay if she was a prisoner. "When it's safe."

Sadness tainted her words. "It may never be safe again."

"I will make it safe for you."

"How?" Her eyes darted back and forth between his. "How can you know that I'm right for you? You hated me only days ago."

"I never hated you, only what you came from." Though, there was a moment where he wanted to hate her. "I don't know how to explain how I know because *I* didn't know so much as *he*," Burne pressed a hand to his chest, indicating his dragon, "knew."

"How can you be sure he doesn't simply want me as his supper?"

"A dragon wouldn't tolerate the drunken affection of his supper." He laughed, even as the beast sent a rumble of disapproval from his chest to her outstretched hand. Sophia didn't look convinced, so he asked, "Do you feel...different around me? Like there is a magnetic pull between us?"

He drew his fingertips from her wrist to the crook of her elbow, nearly groaning as tickling sparks ignited where they connected. "Do you feel this?"

"I tingle when you touch me." She blushed. So, there were subjects that made her shy. "And despite your lack of manners and distasteful sense of humor, I find that I enjoy your company."

A hint of disappointment bit at him. Perhaps she *didn't* feel it as he did. His mother always claimed she was helplessly drawn to his father from the moment they met. Their love was instant. Tender. Anomalous, perhaps.

She interrupted him by adding, "when I thought that you wanted me to stay only while you waited for your mate to make an appearance, I wanted to kill her."

"You are my mate."

"I didn't know that." She glowered at him. "But I was ready to take a dagger to whoever she was and carve out her eyes simply for looking at you."

"You were *jealous*?" He smirked, pleased to have a lighthearted topic to tease her over.

"Lethally so."

"That's how I know." Burne explained, coming back to her original question. "The scent of you makes my mouth water. When I saw you, my heart nearly died from overexertion. If I even think of another man touching you—Gods, just *looking* at you. I want to kill him. I want to rip every appendage off that dared to come near you."

"Are all dragons so violent?"

"When it comes to mates, yes."

"Mates." She hummed wistfully, her hand leaving where it rested over his heart.

"I'm sorry." He said quietly. "I shouldn't have told you now. You need time to grieve. I'll leave you to rest."

He was making his retreat when her hands shot out, gripping his forearm with a touch of panic. "Stay with me?"

Burne hesitated, desperate for some kind of clarity from her. Would she stay? Empathy won out over impatience. Sophia needed comfort. He would give her any comfort she desired.

"Of course." He nodded solemnly, preparing to lay atop the blanket while she was beneath it. Sophia pulled the down layer back before he could settle on it, motioning for him to slip in beside her. This would be a test of his self-restraint if ever there was one.

The sheets were cool beneath him, her clammy skin even cooler. Sophia would need proper attire if she was going to fly with him. He was all too aware of the way the mountain winds could harm a human mate. Burne lifted the blanket up to her shoulders and shimmied in behind her. His body surrounded hers perfectly.

"You're always so warm."

"It's the dragon in my blood."

Burne could hear her smile. "He likes me."

"My dragon?" He snorted. "The beast is enamored with you."

"Big, sweet lizard." She teased, her hand gently caressing his arm. Silence fell around them and her breathing evened. Burne thought she was asleep when she suddenly asked, "will you kill him if you have the chance?"

"Kill who?"

"My father."

He swallowed, tension tugging at the tendons in his throat. "Would you forgive me if I did?"

"I might not forgive you if you didn't."

"Rest, princess." He pressed his lips to her temple. "We can speak of death another time."

"Queen." Sophia mumbled.

"Huh?"

"I am a queen."

CHAPTER 18

BURNE

S OPHIA SLEPT FITFULLY, CRYING out from a dream, her arms thrashing. Burne did his best to calm her, whispering soothing words and running his fingers along her shoulders until she stilled. When she woke her eyes bore weary rings. Red rivers carved lines through the whites around her irises.

"Come with me." He gently coaxed her from the bed, leading her down the hall to a doorway just before the library.

She covered a yawn with the hand that wasn't clasped in his. "Where are we going? Don't you want to break your fast?"

"Later. I have something you need to see."

Burne opened the well-used door to the balcony, carefully leading her down the steep stone steps. It would be a long trek back up on an empty stomach, but it was worth it for the view this time of day. The stairs carried them further and further down until they could feel the shift in elevation. The hall suddenly opened, the walls falling away to reveal a wide covered balcony.

The horizon over the valley was painted deep shades of orange, firelight streaking over the distant hills. Hints of pink touched the edges of clouds where the sun hadn't quite reached her long fingers. Viridescent fields were just visible beyond the foothills, decorated here and there with copses of trees. The forest thickened at the base of the mountain, pine and spruce moving like ocean waves in the morning breeze.

Sophia gasped, wrapping her arms around herself to stave off the biting wind. The mountain air could be bitter in the mornings. Burne sidled up to her as close as he dared, not wanting to assume his welcome simply because she'd asked for him in a moment of grief.

"Calos is the most beautiful place in all the world." She declared, her teeth chattering.

"I haven't seen the rest of the world, but I'm inclined to agree."

"Does it ever get warmer up here?" She rubbed at the goosebumps on her skin.

"Unfortunately, this is warm in the mountains."

Sophia surprised him by taking his arm and pulling it around her like a cloak. She nestled beneath his shoulder and wriggled until she was comfortable. "I never thought I would be envious of a dragon."

"You need not envy. I'll warm you whenever you please."

"How terribly selfless of you."

Burne brought his hand lower to squeeze her hip. "Not at all."

The day seemed slower at this early hour, the sun rising in a glorious, languid stretch. He felt the moments with Sophia in his arms stretching too, giving him a taste of what he hoped she would accept. They could be happy together. Indeed, they might be close to strangers now, but it would be no different than an arranged marriage. Some husbands and wives came to love each other long years after they spoke their vows.

As if reading his thoughts, Sophia asked, "could you fall in love with me, exactly as I am? Or is it merely some force of divinity that draws you to me?"

"I'm half in love with you already."

"I won't hold my tongue for you."

"I should hope you never do."

"I will never be a queen who sits primly at your side and has no purpose other than to smile charitably at her subjects. I wish to be your equal."

"In everything, of course."

"And I want to be kissed." She tilted her chin up. "I don't want to pretend we are chaste until you crawl into my bed at night as if you're ashamed to touch me except with the intention of impregnation."

Burne's eyebrows climbed his forehead. The words caught in his throat. "You—what?"

Sophia turned in his hold, staring boldly at him. "You heard me. I want you to look at me the way you did in your storage room yesterday."

He drew her to him, running his hands down her lower back and pressing her to him. "And how was that?" He whispered, bringing his lips to her ear.

"Like I'm your favorite meal and you've starved for a hundred years."

"You don't want to be kissed, Sophia." She opened her mouth to protest but he cut her off by pinching her bottom lip with his teeth, gently sucking it. "You want to be devoured."

"Yes," she whispered, chasing him with her mouth when he moved away. "Devour me."

Burne obliged her, cupping the back of her head and bringing his lips to hers. It was a forceful kiss, a touch too eager, but her noises of encouragement made it impossible for him to slow. His tongue traced the edges of her mouth and she opened for him. It was as if all the sweetest of her favorite desserts lingered on her tongue. She tasted of sugar and cinnamon, delicious enough to make him growl.

Sophia broke their kiss, panting, "was that a good noise? Or have you decided to eat me after all?"

"I very much want to eat you."

Her eyes widened, the blue half consumed with the black of her pupils. Shuffling steps took her backwards away from him. Burne followed, prowling after her, his body moving the way a predator was meant to. When Sophia bumped into the wall, he dropped his hands on either side of her head, holding his hips against hers and trapping her there. His arousal drew a hard line between them.

When he took her mouth once more, she writhed, maddening him with the teasing movement. He couldn't stop himself from gripping her waist and lifting her up the wall. Sophia's thighs locked around his hips. A moan rose from her throat as he rubbed his length between her legs. Even through their clothes he could feel the heat of her, could sense her heady arousal.

He lifted the fabric of her dress and she gasped his name, leaning away from the wall to press into him. It would be so easy to free himself from his pants and take her right here. And it would be wrong. Making their bond was supposed to be gentle. A consummation of two souls. Burne couldn't bind their hearts and flesh on a windy balcony with nothing but stone beneath her.

Sophia snaked her arms around his neck, squirming in protest when he slowed. "What are you waiting for, dragon?"

"Sophia," his voice was gravel. "This isn't how you should take a maiden."

She objected in a husky whisper. "This is precisely how you should take a maiden."

Any control he'd been clinging to snapped at her words. Burne hoisted her higher, dropping his pants so fast they may have ripped. The apex of her thighs was scorching, a burning temptation. Burne fisted his cock with one hand, using the other to hold her up against the wall. She writhed excitedly as he drew circles in her wetness.

"There's no going back from this, Sophia." He warned her, gritting his teeth to keep from plunging into her with no gentleness. "I don't want you to make a decision in a moment of lust and regret it later."

"You'll be mine?" Her eyes drilled into him, suddenly so serious. "And I will be yours?"

"Yes."

"You won't discard me when you've had your fill?"

It vibrated from his sternum in a growl. "Never."

Sophia widened her legs, taking him an inch into her entrance. Gods, why was she torturing him? "Then I claim you, dragon. You're mine now."

His beast stretched his wings out proudly, filling Burne's head with a victorious roar. He rocked his hips forward, slowly entering her. Every muscle in his body was taut, holding back from the savage need to take her. Her muscles were equally tight, the tension born of pain as much as pleasure.

"Look at me, Sophia." Her eyelids were squeezed shut, lips a hard line. She obeyed, blue flashing at him with warring emotions. "Is it too much?"

"No." She murmured, gently pecking at his mouth. "I only need a moment."

Burne gave her that moment, taking one hand to explore between them. The feel of her stretched around him made his blood pump hotter, if that were possible. He was growing harder inside of her, so unyielding it was almost painful. With one finger he traced her opening, gradually moving higher until he found a spot that made her cry out.

"Do that again." She pleaded.

"Like this, princess?" He circled that sensitive spot, feeling it pulse under his attention.

"Queen." She moaned.

"Like this, my queen?" Burne pulled back and thrust inside of her, his finger keeping rhythm.

Sophia barely managed to whimper out, "yes. Like that."

With each thrust Burne felt the tendrils of a bond, fragile and so very new, reaching out between them. Her pleasure coiled around him, fueling his own and making it nearly impossible to keep from filling her with his seed. Not yet. He didn't want it to be over.

Then Sophia's noises became desperate, rushed and hungry moans. Her body cinched around him, squeezing in a way that made his eyes roll back in his head. This connection truly was divine. Only something crafted by Gods could feel this glorious.

"Sophia," He buried his face in her neck. "Gods, Sophia."

"Make me yours." She begged, clawing at his back.

"You—" He thrust erratically. "Are—" His teeth nipped at the column of her throat. "Mine." Climax hit him with a violent shudder and he sank so deeply into her that they felt as if they were one. The sound that left his throat was bestial, a primal cry of victory and satisfaction.

This wasn't how Burne envisioned the moment he claimed her. He thought of firelight, soft sheets, and slow, sensual caresses. Instead their first coupling was rough and unexpected. He should have anticipated nothing less from Sophia.

He inhaled deeply, trying to capture the scent of her in his lungs forever. A rippling sensation began in his chest, magic stretching and solidifying between them. Effervescent tendrils twined around his limbs, captured his heart, penetrated his very soul. Burne was inside Sophia, but she was inside him too. Her ebbing pleasure tingled in his awareness, as did the tumultuous emotions playing out in her mind.

They were distant and hard to identify, more of a general presence than a clear image.

Dewy eyes lifted to meet his gaze. "I want to do that every day, too." She bit back a grin, hiding her face against his chest. "Twice a day. Maybe more."

"More than twice a day?" He tilted her face back up with a finger to her chin. "What makes you think I have that much stamina?"

"Dragon?" She shrugged.

"I will make love to you as many times as you desire, but I require something of you, too, my demanding queen."

"Fine, it's only fair."

"Tell me what's bothering you." He slipped from inside her, setting her carefully on her feet. "Was it too rough? Did I hurt you?"

Sophia was avoiding his eyes, her boldness diminished. She looked so vulnerable. Fragile. "I am afraid."

"Afraid of what? Nothing should frighten you anymore, you have a dragon at your disposal."

She laughed softly, but the bright noise was fleeting. "I fear you will come to find me insufferable, as others always have. I fear you are wrong about me and I'm just a willing woman soothing your loneliness."

"Foolish." He tsked, taking her in his arms. "Close your eyes, love. Focus inward and pay attention. Do you feel that?" Burne put all his energy into their new bond, sending a surge of affection along the delicate strands of magic. It would take time to strengthen them, time and devotion, but they were unbreakable.

"What is it?" The awe in her voice made him grin. "I don't understand."

"That's our bond. My body is tethered to yours. We're bound now, two parts become one."

"Well, I didn't keep you at bay for very long, did I?"

They both laughed, Sophia's doubts easing away with a breathy noise. Her shivering, however, did the opposite. It was long past time for him to find her some proper mountain attire.

But, if not for her low cut dress, he would never have noticed the mark glittering on her neck.

"Exquisite." He murmured, drawing his thumb over the pale gold dragon visible on her skin.

"What is?"

Burne paused, realizing this was a detail he'd forgotten to mention when telling her about mates. The mark of a dragon bride could appear anywhere. His mother's was somewhere on her midriff and he'd only seen it once when he insisted she show him. It hadn't occurred to him to mention it because for most, they were an intimate secret.

"You bear my mark."

Sophia swiped at her neck. "What does that mean?"

"It means that all will know you belong to me."

She narrowed her eyes. "So, you've marked me like livestock? Or perhaps I'm growing scales?"

"It's much more elegant than that. Come, I'll show you. We can find a mirror while we fetch you some warmer clothing."

"I have a better idea."

CHAPTER 19

SOPHIA

"I WANT TO STAY here forever." Sophia hummed, reclining in the water so she could drift on her back.

"Don't you think you'd get a bit prune-y?"

"Not *here* in this water." She splashed Burne with her foot. "Here in this mountain. I shall be queen of stone and magical pastries. We'll make love until we tire and eat sweet rolls until we're plump."

"A gluttonous queen, then."

"Aren't queens entitled to luxury? My father demands lavish accommodations, as do any of his royal guests. I'm only following their example."

Burne gripped her ankle and pulled her to him. "You're better than that."

"No, I don't think I am." She traced a water droplet down his chest. "I've never done good for anyone but myself. Self-righteousness deluded me into believing I was above all of those fat, greedy lords and ladies. I wallowed in a chamber filled with expensive gowns and silk sheets, gorging myself on roast meats and fancy breads, repeating a story of my own suffering while families starved outside the castle wall."

"And what would you have done? Save for throwing your bread out the window to passing beggars?"

"Killed my brother in his cradle, poisoned my father, and taken the throne?"

"That's dark, love." He chided.

"I'm dark."

"You think you're dark but you, sweet Sophia, are the light Calos needs shining on them."

Anxiety and grief swelled up, nearly drowning her heart, and she turned away from him. "I don't want to talk about this anymore."

Thick arms roped around her, warming her suddenly cold skin and soothing away some of the pain. "We won't speak of it. From this point forward we will worry ourselves with nothing but love making and growing plump."

The water seemed to grow hotter around them. "I thought you said my desires would test your stamina." Sophia teased.

"I'll show you the stamina of a dragon."

Burne moved with startling speed, hoisting her up on the ledge of the pool. Sophia gasped at the jarring change in temperature when her backside hit cold stone. Big hands cupped her legs, easing them apart. Sophia quickly clapped them back together, scowling uncertainly at him.

It was one thing to make love in the morning light on the balcony in a fit of passion. They'd been mostly clothed and Sophia was too distracted to care what he did and didn't see. Even slipping into the pool she felt no modesty. But this? Burne was trying to look at her *there*. What was he doing?

"Don't deny me a taste, Sophia."

"A...taste?" A blush colored nearly every inch of her skin when she realized what he wanted. "Why would you—"

Burne explained by pushing her knees apart and pressing his face to her core. Her thighs reflexively closed around his head, not because of her continued shyness, but because the sudden feel of his tongue sent a jolt through her entire body. By the second stroke she was panting. The third had her head thrown back, legs splayed open, body vibrating with need.

Noises of pleasure echoed loudly through the cavern. Sophia found she was unable to scrounge up the bashful feelings from moments earlier as she cried out. She was too absorbed by the way Burne was teasing her, drawing closer and closer to that delicious pressure point with his mouth. When he finally reached it, his lips closing around her clit, she came undone. A moan came long and low from deep in her diaphragm and she gave herself over to him.

He stepped back from her, licking his lips. The action felt so crude and yet it reignited her hunger for him, sending her sliding back into the pool. The water made her feel weightless, making it easy to wrap arms and legs around Burne's torso and slide down onto his length. His hands came to grip her hips, but he was otherwise motionless as she slowly rode him.

"Beautiful, delicious queen."

Steam was rising rapidly from the water. Sophia paused when she saw a bubble pop at the surface, then another.

"It's getting hotter." So was he, she realized. His skin felt like coals

"My temperature increases when I'm...excited."

"You're not going to boil me alive, are you?"

"As my mate, you're immune to my fire."

"Immune?"

"I'll show you."

Burne cut the conversation off, pushing her back into the wall of the pool and thrusting into her. He followed the same slow pattern she had, his movements harder, his penetration deeper.

The water came to a rolling boil around them. Sweat beaded on all of her exposed skin. Burne's tongue darted out to lick a droplet that sluiced down her neck. The feel of his tongue and the memory of where it had been earlier sent her over the edge, her body squeezing around him. Echoes of her climax carried over the faint bond she was only just becoming aware of.

It rebounded from him as he growled, slamming into her and holding her over him as he filled her with his seed. Absently, Sophia realized that she may be immune to his fire, but she was not immune to becoming pregnant by him.

She'd never envisioned herself as a mother, only because she thought she would one day be married to a hateful man that she despised. By now she was certain she could come to love Burne. Would she want to have his child?

Yes, so long as that child would be safe from her family.

"Why are you angry? Love making is supposed to make you happy."

"Perhaps you did it wrong." Sophia smirked at him.

Burne nipped her breast and he wasn't gentle. "You wouldn't have been making those noises if I did it wrong."

"My mind seems to wander so easily in the direction I don't wish for it to go." She admitted. "My thoughts are disobedient hounds."

"You can't avoid grief, try as you might. It is a living creature inside of you and it demands attention. Just be sure not to feed it and with time it will wither until it's nothing more than a set of bones you pass on occasion."

"You are unexpectedly wise."

"I have my moments."

Sophia sighed, pressing her forehead to his and drinking in the smoky scent of him. Though the water was calming, his skin still felt like molten metal. It should have burned her. The skin of her palms should have blistered, her legs searing as they gripped his hips. How curious that he could burn so hot even as a man. Even more curious that the worst it seemed to do was make her sweat.

And thirst. She was so very thirsty.

"I think we are sufficiently clean and our desires are momentarily sated. Why don't we try some of that plumping up you mentioned?"

She slid from his arms, perching on the edge of the pool and appreciating the cool cave air. "I'm going to look like a plucked chicken when I'm done."

"Good. More of you for me to devour."

CHAPTER 20

BURNE

FOR NEARLY A MONTH, Burne did only three things: feed his mate, make love to her, and sleep. The former made the latter quite necessary. Sophia had a surprising appetite and a very creative imagination. Burne hadn't realized it was possible for his muscles to get so sore.

Sophia was still atop him, the sweat from between her breasts pooling on his chest. Burne absentmindedly traced the lines of her throat, contemplating the best way to broach the topic that was sitting at the forefront of his mind. Each night—and day—had been spent like a wedding night. They fucked and feasted themselves into a stupor. He couldn't deny that he was enjoying himself. More than enjoying himself. Burne had never been happier.

But it had to come to an end. They were only delaying the inevitable and they both knew it.

In between their flares of passion, Sophia grew silent. If not for the bond, he wouldn't have known she was quietly stoking the fires of rage. That rage was building into a hunger that he was all too familiar with. Her heart was becoming vengeful.

They couldn't stay in the mountain forever. It was a lovely dream but it was only that. They each felt an obligation to Calos that couldn't be ignored. They were loyal to their people and leaving them to be ruled by Sophia's brother would only further promote hardship and hunger. George's reign was a destructive force that set Calos on a devastating path.

The people rebelled and the king slaughtered them. Would the remaining subjects submit to that again out of fear? Or would they rise up and destroy their home in a bloody revolution? Burne hoped to prevent both. They deserved better than to live in squalor because they feared their greedy, violent ruler.

Apparently, he wasn't the only one becoming apt at reading the emotions that travelled along their bond. Sophia rolled onto her back, peppering him with questions about dragons and making it impossible for him to say what he planned. It was a rapid change of pace but one that surprised him less now that he understood the way his mate's mind worked. Her brain was almost always whirring, considering half a hundred subjects.

Unless he was inside her. Burne discovered that as a surefire way to pause her overactive mind and give her a much needed distraction. He was selfless, indeed.

"I'm truly immune to you? You can't hurt me?"

"No, you aren't immune to *me*." He explained. "Only to my fire."

"So, you could still strangle me if I become a pest. Or step on me, if I was particularly unlucky."

A growl shook the bed. "My dragon is very unhappy at the suggestion that he would crush you."

Sophia petted his chest, laughing. "Are you a sensitive dragon?"

"There is nothing quite so large and fragile as a dragon's ego." He'd discovered this recently, thanks to his snarky mate.

Finally there was a lull in her questions. Burne rolled, studying Sophia's beautiful, flushed face. Blue irises sparkled back at him, reminding him of the sun on the turquoise waters of the sea to the west. The red of her lips was deeper and more pronounced, probably because he'd been nibbling on them not long ago. He'd noticed a small smattering of freckles along her nose, the kind noble women went out of their way to hide. Burne wanted to lay her in the sun and let the summer rays gild them until they were the most notable feature on her face.

"What are you thinking?"

"That I love each and every one of your freckles."

"What else?" She prodded. "Something has been on your mind."

"You know what it is."

"I'm hungry." She sat up abruptly, slipping from the bed and reaching for her discarded dress.

"Sophia,"

"I think I'll have something with lemon today. Do you like lemon cakes?"

"Sophia." He said more harshly, climbing out of bed after her and securing his arms around her waist. "We can't avoid this forever."

"We can." She whispered. "We can stay here until I'm a wrinkled hag. We have everything we need."

"You mourned for each life that was taken by your father. They are not numbers to bolster your ranks or add taxes to your coffers. You see the subjects of Calos for the people they are."

She turned, pressing her forehead to his chest. "And what am I to do about that? Take the throne from my brother by force? Am I chained to the blood I am born from so tightly that I am doomed to repeat my grandfather's mistakes?"

"Your grandfather took a throne that did not belong to him. The throne of Calos should be yours by birth and marriage. You have more claim than anyone."

"We aren't married."

"We will be." He promised. "As soon as Calos is stabilized we will hold a great feast and honor every person who lives among the city walls."

"What do you suggest then? Shall I fly into the kingdom on the back of a dragon and demand my brother surrender the crown to me?"

"That would be impressive, don't you think?"

Sophia pulled away and finished dressing. She strode to the hearth, crouching before the dying blaze and hugging herself. "I don't like my brother, but I don't hate him either. He's spoiled and lazy. He's also young. How do we know he won't grow into a good king someday?"

"How do you know he won't follow in your father's footsteps?"

"What would happen to him if I usurped his throne? George is petty. He wouldn't capitulate and bow to me. He certainly wouldn't bow to you. What if he used his allies to contest my rule? War will do nothing to fix what is broken in Calos."

"But there are problems to be fixed, you see that much." Burne sat on the arm of the sofa, watching hungry sparks gnaw at the last unburnt bits of wood.

"Of course! I have seen people starving in the streets. Rosemary—" she paused, swallowing thickly. Her pain rushed into him like gale. "Rosemary told me the orphanages were so full they had to turn children away. I want more for my people than that."

"And you can give them more as their queen."

"One more day." She pleaded. "Give me one more day of peace. Then we will choose our next move."

"One more day." He agreed, tugging on a pair of wool trousers that had been strewn across the floor. "But I need to leave the mountain."

"Why?"

"My dragon needs to stretch his wings. He's growing restless. Normally we share forms every day."

"I'll come with you. I'd like to feel a breeze on my face that isn't frigid."

"The wind is colder in flight than it is on the mountain."

"So leave me in the valley. I'll wait for you." Sophia was already preparing for the flight, tugging on the heavy fur cloak he'd found for her.

"Leave you in the valley? We only just finished a conversation about the protective nature of dragons. You know I can't leave you anywhere." He stilled her hand as she tried to fasten a thick brown button.

"You can." Was all she said before marching into the hall.

"Sophia," he growled, chasing after her and enjoying it a bit too much.

"I will not be left alone in a cave for hours while you are afforded the freedom of flight. I want to be under the sun." She put up a finger before he could argue further. "There's hardly going to be bears and wolves about when a dragon is overhead. They're smart predators."

"They aren't the predators I'm worried about."

"If someone comes upon me and dares to threaten the queen of the mountain, I'll scream and you'll eat them." She was already passing through the dining hall and going straight for the cavernous entrance.

Burne wrinkled his nose. "I don't make a habit of eating humans."

"Thieves and rapists don't know that." She patted his arm, her smile as beguiling as it got.

"You are ruthless."

"As a queen should be."

CHAPTER 21

SOPHIA

S OPHIA THOUGHT SHE'D WON the battle over her desire to walk
the valley unaccompanied. As a man Burne understood her unyielding nature. The dragon did not seem to be quite as comprehend-
ing. It took quite a bit of cajoling for the beast to finally fly off, leaving
her to her private thoughts.

"Don't worry, sweet lizard." She stroked the scales on his snout.
He opened his mouth and gingerly took her arm between his teeth,
feigning a bite. Not long ago, having her arm in the maw of a dragon
would have been devastatingly frightening. Now, it only made her
laugh. "You're as fierce as they come. No one would dare threaten me
with you in the skies above."

Reluctantly, Burne stretched those leathery wings and lifted into
the air. What a glorious sight it was. Gilded scales glittered in the
sunlight. The vein and sinew of his wings carved rivers of gold along
the thick skin that made it possible for him to soar. For a moment
Sophia was standing in the center of a tempest, her hair whipping
madly about, her dress feeling as if it might rip away from her body.

Then he was above her, so high above her, that he could have been
a large bird if not for his majestic shape.

She hadn't expected to feel anything other than contempt for
Burne. Maybe pity because it was clear that he was lonely. As she
watched him soak in his freedom, a king reigning over the vast expanse

of blue, she realized how quickly her affection and admiration was turning to a much deeper emotion.

Flickers of doubt pestered her from time to time. Did she feel for him only because the Gods decided it? Their courtship started with a kidnapping and an argument, only to end abruptly with them clambering for each other in a lust haze several days later. Sophia wanted to tell herself that was all it was; lust. Burne was a beautiful man and he possessed quite a skill set when it came to acts of pleasure.

Yet, that wasn't what sent her heart aflutter as she thought of him now. Burne was a good man. Really, truly good. He cared for the people of his kingdom. The throne meant nothing to him if it sat atop the bones of innocents. He wanted it not for the power to rule over others but for the power it would give him to save them.

When Sophia imagined herself as queen, that was how she wanted to rule. It seemed there was no one else in the world that cared to fulfill the role the Gods gave regents. The royalty that ruled the many kingdoms of Svalta hungered for influence and wealth above all else. Their subjects were simply a means to gain those things.

Fate was an interesting lady indeed. It had to be her hand that brought Burne and Sophia together. Perhaps all the Gods were looking down on them, pulling strings in a subtle effort to right some of the wrongs her grandfather had done.

She didn't wish to see harm come to her brother, even if he was a womanizing brat. Would George be forced to give up his inheritance if Sophia returned home wed to a man with a claim to the throne of Calos? Would anyone believe Burne? It was an unlikely story, especially after being fed the fantasy of Saint George for decades.

A breeze rustled through the branches, a whistling sigh. Spruce and tangy pine filled the air, their sticky sap becoming fragrant in the summer sun. Rays dappled the grass beneath her feet, peeking through the branches to smile warmly at her as she made her way to one of the lush green fields that Calos was famous for. Most of the wildflowers had already bolted and dropped their seeds further into the valley where the weather was sweltering. Here, the fields were painted with a rainbow of colors. Purple, yellow, and orange blossoms danced with the grass.

They were lovely and they were heartbreaking, too. Rosemary would pick poppies and arnica for making medicine every summer. There were others, so many plants and flowers that Rosemary knew like the palm of her hand. That was the beauty to be found in death, Sophia supposed. Rosemary's body was gone but she lived on in a thousand soft petals. Her soul lingered in the velvety underside of leaves and the brilliant colors that lit up the verdant fields.

"Be at peace." Sophia prayed. "You are eternal in these blossoms. The summer meadows will pay tribute to you for as long as flowers bloom."

That, more than anything Burne could have said, made her decision for her. Sophia wouldn't be able to live with herself if she let more innocents die to protect her brother's right to the throne. George *could* be a good king, but it was more likely that he would follow the example he was given. Father was a wretched, greedy man. It was his influence that turned George from playful boy to entitled man. Where did the madness end?

A more cynical person might think the answer was with the end of her line. Saint George and his spawn should receive their comeuppance. Despite herself, Sophia was optimistic. She believed she could right the wrongs of her family by working diligently to be a good queen.

It appeared she would be like her grandfather, in some regard. Sophia would usurp the throne of Calos.

The Gods were listening to her heavy thoughts. Not a heartbeat later, the distant rumble of horses could be heard. A black line of riders appeared on the horizon, their attire and the banner they flew unidentifiable from so far away. Sophia tensed, prepared to run back into the trees and call for Burne, when she recognized the blue and grey colors of the king. Not long after, she also recognized the riders as king's men.

It felt too serendipitous that her father's knights appear now, when she had only just left the mountain in over a month. Too coincidental. Sophia stood in the field far longer than she should have, not sure if she planned to face her father's men or hide until she could decide what they wanted. The decision was made for her when she recognized a black beast of a horse and the man sitting atop it.

George was here. Here at the base of Burne's mountain. It didn't make sense.

Sophia lost her chance to flee to the woods as she hesitated at the tree line. They'd spotted her and now it didn't matter how far she went. She couldn't outrun pursuers on horseback and she didn't dare risk drawing Burne back while George was here, not without knowing the reason. Dark horses quickly swallowed up the earth between her and them.

"Sophie!" George shouted her name as he swung from his saddle, his horse continuing on a few paces without him. "Thank the Gods!"

"George, what are you doing? How did you find me?" She stood stiffly as he wrapped her in an uncharacteristic embrace.

"We've been searching for you since you were taken."

"Given," she corrected snidely. "You sacrificed me to the dragon, remember?"

"It was a despicable decision on father's part. He's an old man and he's not right in his head. You're safe now, sweet sister. I've come to rescue you. I've come to slay the dragon." George released her, brushing her hair from her face with a gloved hand. She suddenly realized how grown he was, how quickly he'd gone from leggy boy to powerful man. "I found them, Sophia."

Sophia scowled, still too shocked to find her footing. "Found what?"

"Grandfather's journals." When her scowl only deepened, he shook his head as if he was talking to a slow child and said, "Saint George's journals. I have them. I found them in the catacombs."

Color leeched from her face as it occurred to her what information might have been divulged in those journals. "What does this have to do with me?"

The king's men that accompanied George were shifting restlessly in their saddles, eyes trained upward as if they expected a dragon to dive from the sky. And why shouldn't they? Sophia was taken by a dragon a month ago and was now standing before them, well fed and in one healthy, if not windswept, piece. No one was smart enough to conclude it meant that Burne was what he was—man and dragon—but she suspected that if George knew, so did his men.

"I know how to kill it, Sophia. I know how to kill the dragon."

Sophia made a show of looking around the empty forest. "What dragon?"

George's eyes—as blue and clear as hers—glowed with annoyance. Ah, there was the petulant young boy she'd come to know. "Don't play the fool, sister. You obviously haven't been gnawing on discarded bones in a dank dragon cave. I read Grandfather's journals. All of them. I learned the truth about your *dragon*."

No. Sophia schooled her face, even as her heart hammered madly. *I won't let him repeat history.*

"I don't know what you're talking about. That flying lizard dropped me near a village weeks ago. I've only just decided to walk home."

The expression that took her brother's face was an unfamiliar mask of cold. Precise, calculating. Deadly. "Take her."

Two of the king's guard dismounted at the command, coming for Sophia with muscled arms outstretched.

"I won't go with you." She shook her head, backpedaling. When George gripped her wrist, she twisted it, stumbling back and turning for the forest behind her.

"We *will* be going home together."

"I won't go!" Sophia repeated, weaving between the trees to escape the guards that grabbed for her. They were well trained, legs long and agile, and they corralled her straight into the arms of a third guard. She kicked at them, flailed wildly in their arms, but it was useless. Panic flushed her cheeks and made her body tremble with adrenaline.

Mouth open, Sophia prepared to cry for Burne. The scream died in her throat at the horrible realization that she would be doing exactly what George wanted. If he truly knew how their grandfather killed Burne the First, then Sophia needed to keep her dragon as far from Calos as possible. She wouldn't let her brother hurt Burne.

"You weasel! You spoiled brat!" She shouted uselessly.

"Be careful how you speak to a king, sweet sister." There was a hardness in George's eyes that she didn't recognize. Had she missed this change as she wallowed in her own struggles, or had the arrogant playboy been a well-crafted facade? Sophia couldn't reconcile this frigid, controlled man with the irresponsible younger brother she knew.

"You're not a king."

He took the reins of his horse and gracefully mounted once more. "Oh, but I am." His brief smirk faded into an insincere look of concern. "Our dear father has fallen ill, too grief stricken by your disappearance to get out of bed, and he has stepped down. My coronation happened a week after you left."

"My *disappearance*? You willingly sacrificed me to a dragon! Lies and nonsense. All of it!"

"No, Sophia. It's true. Our poor king couldn't take the thought of harm coming to you. Not after the shock of that ill planned rebellion. It was too much. I had to handle it. That is my duty as king." George leaned forward in his saddle, grinning. "Now I need something from you, sister."

"I'll do nothing for you. Not while you have me detained like a prisoner."

"You are my prisoner and you will be until you bring that dragon to me."

"He's not a hound that will come when I whistle." Lie. Burne would come if she called to him. She was silently praying that he wasn't already rushing this way.

"You and I both know that's not true. Not if I'm to believe what grandfather wrote in his journals. There are some *very* interesting truths about dragons in those accounts." George waggled a leather journal in his right hand. "Why did the dragon let you go, Sophia? Why hasn't it eaten you? And why do you look so well fed? So clean and cared for? So *sated*?"

"It left me here." A poorer lie than the last, but she was beginning to feel trapped.

George made a gesture toward his guards and one of them yanked her hair back, tilting her head painfully to reveal her neck. "Ah, but what's this? I don't remember you bearing a birthmark, sister."

Her mark. Of course. It was damning. "It's nothing."

"Call the dragon, Sophia."

"I can't."

"Can't or won't?"

"Can't."

"Very well." He tucked the journal back into his saddle bag. "Do you want to know the very first thing I did when I was crowned king?" He fussed idly over his fingernails, looking bored. "I took that servant of yours to the town square and had her hanged for treason. Her son too. And all those other traitorous bastards that dared speak against their rightful king."

"You—" Sophia wanted to vomit. Her body shook with rage and disgust. "You killed them? All of those innocent people? *My people?*"

How was this possible? How was this the brother she'd watch grow from a toddling, motherless boy?

"Innocent? They were traitors to the crown. I rid the world of filth."

She loosed a mournful scream. "You murderer! How could you? You are not the rightful king! You don't deserve to rule over the people of Calos!"

George's grin widened. He'd gotten what he wanted from her. The two guards bound her hands and feet, tossing her over the back of a horse as she screamed and bucked. Just as they took off at an uncomfortable pace, her body bouncing painfully atop the horse, a dragon's furious screech sounded overhead. A shadow passed over them and a glittering gold body appeared in the sky.

Burne would have come whether or not she'd screamed. Sophia was foolish to demand a walk to herself, even if she'd so desperately wanted to clear her head. He was coming for her because he felt her grief, her outrage and fear, just as Sophia felt his fury. He would burn every man and beast here to ashes. He would destroy the entire kingdom to get to her.

That was what Sophia was afraid of.

CHAPTER 22

SOPHIA

"STAY AWAY! DON'T HURT innocents for me!" Sophia screamed up to the sky as she was thrown over the back of a horse.

She hadn't a clue if Burne would listen. If their places were reversed, she wasn't sure that she would obey him. Only her faith in his dedication to the people of Calos, to keeping them safe and not crushing down the walls, trampling people in a mindless hunt, helped steady her.

It did nothing for the wild pounding of her heart. That could be blamed on the gloved hand that rested tightly on her rump. There were far better places to hold her steady as the horse turned, jostling her madly atop the guard's lap. Several snickers carried over the sound of horse hooves. Sophia craned her neck to look up, making note of each and every guard that took part in her humiliation. Their faces would not be forgotten.

Calos was a half hour ride from the mountains at a good pace, longer if you were trying to lure a dragon that was stubbornly staying high overhead. George must have let his men in on the secret he discovered. They all seemed remarkably calm considering that Burne was stalking them with lethal intent. Unfortunately, his distance and obedience to her word only proved that George was right.

Nausea rolled through her stomach. History was repeating itself. Violent, terrible history.

No, it wouldn't be the same. Sophia would not let Burne sacrifice himself for her. She wouldn't go peacefully or quietly along with her brother's plans, whatever they may be.

Burne remained above them the entire journey home, circling and occasionally swooping low in an attempt to get a better view of her. He was prudent, unsure of the situation and not ready to take a risk. Would George hurt her? Could they have a knife at her back? Sophia didn't have the answer to either question.

All of her was a boiling rage, so hot it made her lower belly feel as if it was on fire. Was it her own fire or his sparking inside of her?

By the time they rode up to the city gates, Sophia's body ached. Bruises were no doubt blooming on her hips where they bounced mercilessly against the saddle. Her muscles were too taut, the tension building within her pulling them viciously. George's horse was barely at a standstill before he leapt to the ground, coming for Sophia with fury in his gaze.

"Bring it here!" His hands fisted at his sides, red creeping up his neck, and his lips were puckered in an angry pout that so resembled their father. She was reminded of George at three years old, demanding that Rosemary leave him alone and bring their mother back. He'd been too young to grasp that she was never coming back.

"I can't, George."

He gripped her arm and wrenched her from the horse. There was no way to catch herself with her hands bound. Grass rose to meet her, the ground unforgiving on her sore body. "You can!"

"He's a dragon. How do you expect me to summon him?"

"You *told him* to stay away."

"Did I?" With effort, Sophia picked herself up off the ground. She made a show of dusting grass and debris from her skirts. "And you think that flying lizard actually listened to me?"

"I know what he is, Sophia. Don't play games with me." He lifted her arm to poke her in the rib. "You're plump and unharmed. How is that possible? I expected that you would become the newest in a collection of bones somewhere up in the mountains by sundown."

"Brother dearest, I'm hurt. You sent me off to be dragon dinner?" She pouted. "I thought I was to be his bride."

"You were. You *are.* Now call him down here so I can kill him and make my claim as king. I'll not have you shaming me in front of those treacherous beggars again!"

"I can't." George slapped her across the face. "I *won't.*"

His grip on her arm became crushing. Sophia grit her teeth to keep from crying out. Unsatisfied with her silence, he twisted, bringing her to her knees. Every part of her wanted to fight, to wrench her arm away, but his hold was unyielding, as was the rope around her wrists. Finally, she gave in, crying out as white briefly flashed across her vision. Any further and George would break her arm.

Burne let out an answering cry, bellowing his violent intent into the clouds. That reaction was damning.

George smirked, his eyes twinkling. Only the cruelty written in those eyes made him look the man he was becoming and not the boy. Her brother was nineteen, on the cusp of manhood but cursed with a pert nose, cherubic cheeks, and glossy brown hair that flopped messily around his face. In fits of laughter he sounded young, too young to be mere years away from becoming a king.

"I'm growing impatient, sister."

"You were born impatient." She managed to grunt.

Another cry as he pushed her arm past it's limit. Sophia heard a groan, sure it was something permanently breaking. *"Call him down!"*

"No," was her last choked word before the pain became too much and her consciousness blinked out.

CHAPTER 23

SOPHIA

WATER DRIPPED LAZILY FROM somewhere overhead and for a heartbeat, Sophia thought she was back in the mountain with Burne, waking from a terrible nightmare. Almost immediately, she came to her senses. If Burne were here, she wouldn't be so cold. Her body wouldn't ache. The dress clinging to her clammy skin would be dry. No, it would be gone and she would be pressed comfortably against that hot forge of a chest.

All she felt against her now was the uncompromising bite of stone. Its uneven surface jutted into her hip, making her already deep bruises throb. She rolled, trying to ease the pressure only to cry out in pain as her weight pressed onto her left arm. Gingerly, she traced her fingers along the arm, prodding at the most painful point, where her upper arm met her shoulder. Her head momentarily swam. Was it broken? She didn't know how to tell.

The arm hung awkwardly at her side, too limp, and it didn't seem to rotate as it should when she dared move it. Whatever George had done, it didn't feel as though it would heal without attention. Sitting upright was a struggle with only one good arm. Even then, her eyes had scarcely adjusted to the dark surroundings and she couldn't immediately find a wall to prop herself up against.

Even that much exertion took the breath from her. A very bad sign.

As she came to her senses, Sophia became aware of a rabid pulse in her middle. It was Burne, raging and panicked. Miraculously, he hadn't come barreling through the castle wall. Perhaps that was because he'd heeded her plea. Or perhaps it was because he was foolish enough to do as George demanded and was ready to walk right through the gate and sacrifice himself on her part. Sophia would be furious with him.

She shifted positions, doing her best to rest her arm and focus her mind on anything but the pain. Could Burne feel how much she ached? Calm didn't come to her easily, not when she finally grasped where she was, but she tried for it. Collected, patient, ready to do what it took to wait out her brother until he came to see reason.

Ha! George was very unlikely to see reason.

A reasonable brother did not lock his sister in the dungeon. A *reasonable brother* didn't offer her to a dragon for the sake of his reputation. George was not a child any longer. He was a tyrant in the making, cruel and violent. If he was allowed to rule, he would bring Calos to destruction.

Was there no one left that would hear her out? No one left who would stand for justice? Or had George scared them all into submission? Sophia pondered their father. Did the king—George was no king, not now and hopefully not ever—know that his only daughter was injured and freezing in a dank cell?

"Hello?" She called tentatively. If George had stationed one of his guards down here, she wasn't sure what their response would be. Would he allow them to torture her? To...violate her?

No. She had to believe her brother was better than that, at least.

"Hello?" She raised her voice. "I need an audience with the king!"

"The king is not taking audience." A disembodied voice echoed down a seemingly endless hall.

In all her time living in the castle, Sophia had been to the dungeon only once. She was a girl, desperate to prove herself to the other daughters of the court. They insisted she wasn't brave enough to venture down here. Even as a child, her ego couldn't take being called a coward, so down she went. The stone steps were steep and boundless. Deeper and deeper she climbed, wondering if perhaps this wasn't the staircase to the dungeon but the staircase to hell.

Around her, the air grew colder, moist and foul smelling. Eventually she found herself standing in a long, dark hallway. Half a dozen torches provided the only light, barely enough to see cell after cell. Why did a castle need such a big dungeon? As far as she knew, they rarely had prisoners. To this day, Sophia didn't know who the moaning, beseeching voices belonged to.

One man groaned a plea, followed by another. Soon there were too many to differentiate, a chorus of misery that haunted her all the way back up the steps. She was breathless and terrified until that very last landing. There she paused to catch her breath and let the color return to her face. Sophia faced the other girls with perfectly schooled features, playing the role of brave princess better than she expected.

They still wouldn't accept her.

If she could go back to that day, Sophia wouldn't have cowered. She would walk the hall, learn the layout, discover what secrets lived down here. Perhaps there was a way of escaping, even if it meant tricking the guard. The thought of seducing him made her feel filthy, but if it was the only way to save herself and Burne—to save Calos—she might have to. Though, with a glance down at her twisted arm, she realized that she was in no shape to fool a guard. She'd be lucky if she could walk out of here when they freed her.

If they freed her. George had no reason to. Even if he killed Burne—A shudder took her and she decided not to pursue that thought. Regardless of what happened, George had no use for her.

Sophia leaned her head back against the stone with a heavy sigh. It was cool and made her hair feel surprisingly damp. At least it was a distraction from her shoulder. Now that her eyes were adjusting to the darkness, she took in her current home. There was a nest made of crushed up, old hay in one corner. Another held a bucket that, by the look and smell, wasn't thoroughly emptied and cleaned between prisoners. Actually, each cell that Sophia could make out through the bars seemed freshly disturbed.

Of course. This was where George must have put the rebels before he murdered them all. The dungeon saw more use in the last month than it had in years.

Sophia dragged herself to the scratchy pile of hay, taking extra care to protect her left arm before lying down. It was terribly uncomfortable and likely full of fleas but she found a sense of comfort resting her head in the same place that Rosemary had rested, if only for a moment. Poor, sweet Rosemary. And that young man with his red cloth. All of them were innocent. Needlessly killed by her brother.

Not long ago Sophia, had pondered a peaceful resolution to this all. She'd thought it possible to negotiate with George or at least find some way to occupy him. He seemed such a simple boy, easily distracted by women and wealth. Perhaps she should have spent more time paying attention to her little brother's ambitions.

Now, it seemed impossible to resolve this without violence. Without death.

The question was, would it be her death or would George force her hand and forfeit his own life?

CHAPTER 24

SOPHIA

THAT DRIPPING. THAT GODS-AWFUL dripping. Sophia didn't know how long she'd been in the dark. Several days, at least. Could it be longer? Impossible to tell when there was no sunrise or sunset. No sunlight at all. The lack of light wasn't just confusing, it was demoralizing. No one had come to speak with her. George made no more demands. Maybe he'd already forgotten she was here.

She was given two meals a day, each consisting of the same stale bread and the same meat slop. She was fairly certain it was the unwanted trimmings that usually went to the dogs. The scent alone made her stomach into a churning sea of discomfort. The single bite she'd attempted on the first day sent her running to the corner to vomit in the waste bucket. Even when the tray of food was removed by a faceless prison-keeper in black, the nausea lingered.

More than once, Sophia began to worry that the injury to her arm was worse than she realized. There was no laceration in the skin for infection to creep in, yet she was inexplicably ill. Even when she woke from a night—or what she thought was night—of rest, exhaustion overtook her again quickly. Often, she would sit by the bars, calling out and waiting for someone—anyone—to speak with her, only to doze off in her upright position.

There was no fever that she could tell, but her stomach was bothersome most of her waking hours. Thinking of the luxurious food she'd dined on with Burne and imagining it in place of the bread and meat gruel only made her feel sicker. Lemon tarts? Sweet buns? Apple crumbles? If she were to say them aloud, she was sure she would lose what little contents her stomach held.

Gods, this place was misery. If Sophia ever became queen—*when* she became queen—her first order of business would be to collapse the stairwell leading to the dungeon. She had no need to keep prisoners locked away when she could simply feed them to her dragon.

The longer she was down here, the more she wanted to feed her brother to the dragon too.

BURNE

Madness was going to take Burne if he didn't act soon. Eleven days had passed since Sophia's brother took her. How George ended up at the base of the mountain and why Sophia didn't call for help, Burne hadn't yet discerned.

At first, a dark, bitter part of himself felt tricked. It was a brief moment of weakness and a shameful one, but he did wonder if Sophia planned this. Another wicked villain from Saint George's bloodline trying to take down the dragon.

Why would she, though? When she now had a devoted dragon at her beck and call. When her grief was so real. Her affection so real.

And her pain. That was real too and every breath he took without fixing it nearly matched her agony.

"Stay away," She'd told him. *Stay away.* How could he stay away when she was suffering? When he didn't know where she was or what was happening to her?

The sole reason he hadn't rushed into the city, tearing apart buildings in search of her, was the gentle calm she sent his way day after day. Sophia was hurt but it was not growing worse. They weren't tormenting her.

Well, that was his *main* reason for doing as she'd asked. The other was that he knew how this scenario ended. Burne was ready to lay down his own life for his mate and his kingdom, but he couldn't do that to her. He thought of his mate throwing herself from the queen's tower in despair and wanted to tear his skull open to rip out the offending thought.

Maddening. All of this was maddening and he only had so much restraint left.

For eleven days George had Sophia and for eleven days Burne took to the skies above Calos, trumpeting his challenge for the would-be king. What was his plan? To keep his sister hostage until he'd been crowned, and she was no longer a threat to his title? Or was it more sinister?

Burne couldn't shake the niggling feeling that George hadn't taken Sophia over a rivalry for the throne. Why bother when she was already gone, stolen by a dragon? If he understood what Burne was, however... Gods, how could he? The history of Burne's family was forgotten by Calos.

And yet, it was the only conclusion that made sense. Thus, it was the reason Burne would have to be cunning.

So far, he'd contemplated several options for stealth entry into the inner kingdom. Shepherds were allowed outside the walls to tend to flocks, if they weren't already living in cottages in the valley. No one else dared leave the relative safety of stone structures while an angry dragon was about. More than once he thought of knocking out a shepherd and stealing his clothes—a naked man could hardly walk through the gates—but had no idea what would happen next. A shepherd couldn't march up to the castle and demand to know where the princess was.

There was also scaling the wall, killing the guards and storming in, or landing atop the castle and shifting forms there. The problem he ran into over and over again was that he wouldn't know where to find Sophia once he was inside. Confronting George would be the simplest course of action but then he would have to reveal himself. What would stop George from threatening Sophia? She was the perfect bargaining chip and Burne feared George knew that. Each day without her made his dragon more unruly, hungrier for violence.

The need to be near his mate, to protect her, was stronger than even his need to eat. To sleep. The Gods gave his kind mates to balance them and in doing so created monsters that would destroy the world for the woman fate chose for them. Reckless, foolish Gods.

The sun was rising on the twelfth day when any chance for mercy vanished. Pain screamed across the bond between them, a bolt of lightning that struck with such violence that he shifted instantly. Wings burst through the canopy of the young copse he'd been hiding beneath. Two shepherds screamed, their voices matching the panicked bleating of their sheep.

They should be afraid. They should all be very, very afraid. Burne bugled a war cry into the dawn, a challenge for the would-be king who dared harm Sophia.

Crimson and orange light colored the horizon. To Burne, it looked like bloodshed and fire. So much fire. There would be plenty of both by the end of this day.

Chapter 25

Sophia

F OR WHAT FELT LIKE endless days and nights, Sophia was ignored. Someone left a tray of food for her, what she assumed
was twice a day. A bucket of clean water came once. The water she
gulped as if she'd been wandering the desert. The food mostly made
her stomach turn. She felt ill all the time but thankfully she was void
of fever and chills.

Distantly, she thought she heard the sound of a dragon roaring
overhead. It happened infrequently but she was beginning to wonder
if *that* marked the beginning of a new day. Sophia could picture Burne,
his heart filled with nothing but wrath as he flew above the kingdom
to trumpet a challenge for her brother.

Perhaps today George would finally answer that challenge. Instead
of a tray of cold, greasy meat and dry bread, Sophia was greeted by a
man in long brown robes. A healer, one of few who still resided in the
kingdom. Father hadn't seen need to fund their house of healing so
that they could take on more apprentices. Why bother when his own
personal healer was young and well paid? The people of Calos couldn't
afford healers anyway.

Long ago, they used to treat anyone and everyone for free. Sophia
had learned that in one of Burne's many books. The house of healing
only began requiring a fee because the king refused to offer them the

gold required to treat the sick and procure the rare herbs needed for valuable medicines.

"What is your name?" Sophia decided the best course of action was to be wary but polite. She was in dire need of an ally.

The healer did not respond as the guard closed the cell door, locking him in with Sophia as if she were a dangerous prisoner who might attack and escape at any moment.

"Are you here to fix my arm? Has my brother sent you?" More silence answered her echoing queries.

Cold hands prodded her useless arm until she cried out. The healer made a rasping sound in his throat, his gaze downcast as he considered her injury.

"Please," Sophia begged. "At least tell me what's going on."

His eyes were a limpid green when they turned up to her. It was a brief glance, swimming with guilt and apology. More than that, it was filled with fear. He gave the subtlest shake of his head and she understood.

Then, with no warning, the healer grabbed her wrist and jerked her arm out straight in front of her. Pain screamed along her shoulder, matching the scream that left her lungs. There was a loud pop and suddenly her arm was mobile again. So terribly sore, but she could move it better than she'd been able to since George wrecked it.

Not two minutes later, dust rained from the ceiling and the walls shook. A horrible, violent roar came from somewhere above. Again and again Burne sounded his fury over Calos. More debris sprinkled over their heads. Perhaps he was doing more than *voicing* his anger.

"Fuck, he's going to bring the whole place down." The guard ripped the cell door open, shooing the healer out and taking Sophia by the arm. Mercifully, it was her uninjured arm.

The journey from the dungeons was long, longer than she remembered it being. Each step caused her to stumble all over again, the guard moving too fast and not bothering to help her stay upright. Several times she pitched forward, her knees scuffing painfully on stone. An eternity passed before the stairs ended in a too bright hall.

"What took so long?" The expression on George's face was thunderous, but the voice he used still sounded so childish. A boy demanding his dessert when he hadn't finished dinner.

"She tripped on every step." Sophia was tossed to the ground, her shoulder smarting as she caught herself on her hands.

"I've grown tired of waiting, dear sister."

Sophia glared up at him. "Waiting for what? Your testicles to drop?"

A sound that was distinctly amused snorted from the guard's nose before he could stop himself. George glowered at him and pointed an angry finger at Sophia. "Do it."

The side of her face burned as a rough hand slapped across it. A second slap brought her back to her knees. The third threw her onto the ground, her head smacking into stone.

"Enough." George waved a hand to halt the guard. "I could have let them hurt you, you know. I could have let them do much worse than this."

"And you could have been born a worm and you would be more charming."

The guard behind her broke into a fit of chuckling coughs.

Another slap, this one from George. "Call down the dragon before he destroys this entire kingdom."

"Or what?"

"Fine." He lifted her from the ground by her hair. "I gave you a chance to do what is right for your kingdom. Instead you chose that creature. *Dragon's whore.*"

Pain burned her scalp with every step that George dragged her. And each time she winced, Burne's roar echoed frighteningly above them.

Please. She begged him and perhaps the Gods too. *Please don't be reckless. Don't let history be repeated.*

Their courtship was swift and disastrous, but as she marched to what could very well be her death, the monstrous presence of Burne overhead, she realized she loved him. They were kindred spirits, brought together by Lady Fate not only to love each other but to dream of a better world. To make that dream come to fruition. Determination became a fire in her veins, roaring hotter than the pain in her shoulder, the throb where chunks of hair were nearly ripped from her scalp. For a moment Sophia imagined that this was what it felt like to be a dragon. A beast roared within her and molten power blazed in her heart.

Don't give up. She whispered to Burne, hoping he could feel her determination across their burgeoning bond. *Fight him. For me. For your people.*

George dropped his hand from her head to her weak shoulder when they cleared the castle and stepped into the morning sun. Several more king's guard, encased in black leather armor, came to flank them as they made their way out of the castle gates and through the streets of Calos. The last time Sophia was marched down these streets, she was wrapped prettily in chiffon and lace, a red sash marking her fate. Now she was filthy, her skin exposed in the torn, thin gown she wore.

There were no sneering courtiers to watch her, but citizens who had already paused in their work to observe the dragon began to follow them. They left their homes and shops, even abandoned their carts to walk silently behind her. George had the good sense to look nervous when a flock of peasants surrounded his guards.

"People of Calos!" He addressed them loudly, rushing her to the gate. "My sister has returned with the dragon. She intends to burn this kingdom to the ground to get revenge for making her the dragon's bride. As your king, it is my duty to protect you from this threat of destruction, as my grandfather once protected you. Watch as I end this beast once and for all."

The few who stood by and warily eyed them as Sophia passed were suddenly very interested. Murmurs of confusion rippled through the crowd. A handful were brave enough to shout insults at George.

"Murderer! Liar!" They called.

George bared his teeth, free hand clutching the hilt of the short sword he wore on his belt. It was ornamental, weighted down with jewels and gold. Could he even lift it on his own? Or did it take a trio of servants to strap it to him?

Half of Calos trailed them out of the gates and back up the hill where Burne had first come for her. George barely shouted one word before Burne was careening in a downward spiral, landing so violently that the ground shook and several guards lost their footing. Screams of fleeing people were drowned out by a ferocious, angry bellow. Burne ended his war cry close enough to the first line of guards that his teeth nearly scraped their drawn swords. Two soldiers broke the line, one fainted. A fourth pissed himself, the liquid trickling down the armor strapped to his thigh.

The onlookers that were brave enough to stay kept a safe distance, hopping nervously from foot to foot at the bottom of the hill. Sophia could see them straining to hear as George demanded, "Show us what you really are, dragon."

Burne growled, smoke rising from his nostrils.

Voice trembling, George demanded again, "Show us your true form! I know what you are."

"Don't give him what he wants." Sophia pleaded, seeing the conflict in those shimmering golden irises.

George upped the ante, drawing a dagger from his belt and pressing it to his sister's throat. "Keep your mouth shut, Sophia."

"You would kill your own sister?"

"If that's what it takes to secure my crown." He hissed. "I owe you nothing. What have you done for me, but mock and meddle? Refuse courtship and make a nuisance of yourself?"

"I shouldn't have to *do* anything to earn your love, brother." Quieter, she said, "You always had mine."

George ignored her remark, as heartless and uncaring as the picture Burne painted of their grandfather. "Make him reveal himself and I won't hang his body from the parapets like I did Rosemary. Maybe I'll even let you bury him." He wanted her to struggle, to fight him and enrage Burne.

It worked. Sophia thrashed, screeching at the vile creature the Gods gave her for a brother. Immediately she felt the bite of steel, a warm ooze as blood poured down her neck.

Burne made a noise that sounded far too much like surrender. George pressed the dagger closer, drawing more blood. Sophia took in her situation and in a sudden rush of clarity, knew what had to be done. There was only one true way out of this and she saw it as clear as she saw the sun against the blue sky. Though her heart ached for the younger brother she once had, it was clear that George was something else entirely now. Something too wicked to rule over innocent people.

"Get back!" Sophia croaked. "Please, get back if you want to live." Most of the crowd obeyed. Some did not. "Fine." Her throat was raw. "Fine, brother. See what hatred brings you."

If her mind hadn't already been made up, the triumphant smile he flashed her sealed their fates forever.

"Do it." Her eyes bored into Burne's, even as she begged the Gods to forgive her this choice. "Do it, Burne. For your people."

There was a moment where the entire world seemed to still. Clouds froze midair, the grass lost its breezy sway. Even the breath from the gathered crowd ceased to move. Burne lowered himself, golden eyes steady, head hovering just above the ground. His jaw came open with a swift crack and hiss. The air shimmered hotly around him.

Then everything vanished from view as a brilliant inferno engulfed Sophia and her brother.

CHAPTER 26

SOPHIA

THE SMELL OF COOKED meat filled the valley, the air thick with grease. Charred bodies littered the ground around her feet when the flames cleared and Sophia couldn't stop herself from retching. At least the acrid scent of vomit covered the other odors.

George was nothing but a crumpled pile of bones and ash. Sophia stared down at him, waiting for the guilt to strike her. It didn't. Sadness was a deep lake in her belly as she realized her brother was well and truly gone but she knew there was no other way. One death to prevent hundreds.

Most of his guards had perished too. Thankfully, none of the crowd of onlookers were too badly harmed. The few who hadn't heeded her warning and backed away had sooty faces, some singed hair and clothing. Burne had been careful with them. She wondered if any of them recognized that.

Smoke snaked from half a dozen places on the ground, whispering around her bare body. Through the haze she spotted glowing eyes, black slit pupils focusing so intently on her that she thought perhaps there was still a chance she would melt.

Molten gold, as hot and lethal as the fire that burned around her moments ago. That was what she was looking at. It consumed her, swallowed her up until she was nothing, saw nothing—*felt* nothing—but him.

Then she was abruptly pulled back to the surface by a pair of bony hands. They rested delicately on her upper arm. A wizened woman was attached to them at the wrist. Her eyes, so wide Sophia couldn't judge the color, darted between the dragon and the thin shawl she was wrapping around Sophia's shoulders. It was threadbare and scratchy, but Sophia welcomed it when she noticed that her clothes were reduced to ashy dust.

"Thank you." Sophia murmured.

The woman only dipped her head, bowing low and staying there. Another woman approached, her face filthy but youthful. She untied an apron from her waist and carefully fastened it around Sophia. She bowed as well.

Another two people braved the hill, their heads craning to keep Burne in their view. They bowed too.

More and more came, dozens, then hundreds. Some were dirty, many looked hungry, all bore the same look of cautious hope. Even fear of the nearby dragon didn't stop them from pouring out of the city gates.

The citizens of Calos stood before her, silently taking in the horrors at her feet. They should have called her a murderer. King killer. She killed her own brother, called for his death. Instead, they were offering their fealty, their loyal, their *faith*.

Burne shifted, provoking startled gasps from several women. The man closest to him wobbled on his knees. The dragon paid them no mind, though. His focus was still fixed solely on Sophia as he stepped before her and lowered his head in a reverent bow.

Murmurs of awe rippled around her. Someone shouted, "Long live queen Sophia," and it was echoed by a male voice. A ripple of speakers answered the cry until every last person was shouting it, their fists raised in triumph. "Long live Queen Sophia!"

Tears carved trails through the soot coating Sophia's face, but she kept her chin high, shoulders back. The mixed collection of cloth barely covered her body as she stood before the people of Calos, *her people*, and bid them rise. She waited until no man, woman, or child was on their feet, then she took her own bow, as deep as her coverings allowed without exposing too much.

"I am humbled by you and I promise to serve you every day until my life shall end. I promise to offer peace where you have been given violence, to offer prosperity where you have been given poverty, and to see joy where there was despair." Sophia pushed a smile, giving the people what they needed to see.

Burne reached out a clawed hand and she climbed carefully into it. The next moment they were airborne and the people shrank until they were colored specks, shouting their shock and awe. When Sophia was flying with Burne in a gown and a cloak, the wind was cold. With neither, she felt like she was being pelted with imperceptible shards of ice.

The torment ceased as quickly as it had begun as Burne carefully settled her atop the castle, just beyond the ramparts. Stone rumbled and shook under his weight and her newly discovered relief vanished as she feared the roof would cave in beneath them and they would tumble into the throne room. Before her fear could be realized, Burne was shrinking down, shimmering golden scales becoming tan skin. His muscles were taut with fury and tension when he engulfed her, pressing her so tightly to his chest that she wheezed.

Sophia didn't care if she suffocated, so long as she was suffocating in him. The scent of smoke clung heavily to him, but it was a comforting, familiar scent. Nothing like the odor in the valley below. His skin was blessedly warm and she pressed closer, if that was possible.

Thick, trembling fingers came behind her head, cradling it to him as he murmured her name over and over.

"I'm never letting you out of my sight again."

"What if I have to relieve myself? I won't have you following me to the washroom."

His laughter was all relief and no humor. "You're unharmed, then?"

"Not exactly, no." Sophia winced just as she remembered her injured shoulder. It throbbed back into awareness, grinding painfully in his embrace.

Blinding gold seeped into the murky brown of his irises, forcing her to blink and turn away. "I would kill him twice if I could. I would roast him slowly, until his insides began to cook while he still lived. "

She gaped at Burne, feeling his fury, understanding it. Yet, despite the harm done to her, to her people, George was her brother. They shared the same blood. Nausea bubbled her already empty stomach and she whirled in time to keep from spewing all over Burne. He gripped her hair, brushing it away from her face as she gagged over and over again. There wasn't even air to be released from her belly by the time she was done.

"I'm sorry, love. I'm so sorry."

"It wasn't wrong, what you did." She whispered. "But the Gods will judge me as they see fit."

They stood atop the stone structure that shadowed over Calos, holding each other until Sophia was shivering despite Burne's warmth. It took several minutes of convincing—threatening, actually—to get him to shift back into the dragon and fly away. Unless he was content to reveal his nature to the entire kingdom, it wouldn't do for the dragon to land up there and then disappear, only to be replaced by the queen's mysterious betrothed.

Burne took off into the sky, impressive wings nearly knocking her off her feet as they beat the air. Sophia described a hidden entrance in the wall, near the kitchens, where Burne could return through. She wasn't sure how she planned to explain his presence or their engagement. There were a thousand tasks she would have to complete, and soon, but she didn't yet have the mental strength for them.

The only three she could focus on in that moment were getting inside, finding clothing, and hunting down her father. As for the rest? They would have to be sorted out tomorrow.

Tomorrow. She silently promised herself over and over as her mind whirred so rapidly it threatened to fly right out of her skull.

Sophia carefully climbed down the stone steps that led to a guard station. The Gods were smiling upon her. The dank room and the hallway leading to the two west facing towers were empty. Even the guards seemed to have vacated their posts to watch the drama with the dragon. They would be returning soon and it wouldn't do for the queen to be caught half-naked and filthy in their station.

Her bare feet clapped a quiet pattern on the frigid stone floors as she raced down hallway after hallway, desperately seeking her old chambers. Hopefully her father hadn't already cleared away her things.

Burne was already reclining on her bed when she flung the heavy chamber door open. "How did you—?"

"I scaled the wall."

"You—Gods, what would people say if they witnessed that? It's not every day that naked men climb through my window and into my bed."

He growled deep in his chest. "I should hope for their sake no man has ever tried to climb into your bed."

"Many have tried. Only you have succeeded, beautiful lizard." Her lip trembled through her smile, fresh tears clouding her vision.

Burne was off the bed in a heartbeat, scooping her into his arms and carefully carrying her to the adjoining room. A deep tub waited clean and empty in the corner. He twisted the metal valve that opened the faucet and hot water splashed loudly onto porcelain.

Sophia watched the water level rise, occupying her overloaded mind by wondering how it was that the water stayed hot as it traveled through the pipes. She knew it was fed by hot springs that boiled somewhere below the castle, but until she watched Burne heat water with his own body, she'd never considered the logistics of it.

He wasn't going to let her waste her time puzzling it out right then. Burne lowered himself into the tub, carefully laying her across his lap without disturbing her shoulder. A hiss escaped her lips as the water rose around her aching body. It was too hot. She welcomed the discomfort, letting it burn away some of her grief and fear.

There was so much fear. Fear that she would fail as a queen, fear that she would be damned for the death of her brother. She feared that Burne wouldn't be accepted by the people of Calos. The worst of the fears was the one that haunted her each and every day that she spent rotting in the dungeon. It wasn't possible, not anymore, but she couldn't shake it. What if Burne had died? What if he'd given his life to save hers? She wouldn't allow it. Not today, not ever.

"I thought you were so bitter," she whispered as he gently washed soot and grime from her skin. The water around them was already black. "You were spiteful. I planned on hating you for as long as you kept me captive, perhaps longer."

"You were never a captive."

"Maybe not." She twisted, meeting his eyes, her voice fierce. "I was very wrong about you, Burne. You're a beautiful, good-hearted soul. You are the ruler this kingdom deserves—desperately needs." Tears, there were still so many tears in a rush to escape down her cheeks. "And

I need you too, desperately. You must make me a promise." She cupped his face in earnest. "Promise me you won't lay down your life for me. I could never live with it. I thought that I would hate you forever, but I don't. I love you and I feel as if my heart would cease to beat and my lungs would no longer breathe without you."

Burne kissed her, tenderly, carefully. "I can't make that promise, my sweet Sophia. You are my heart and my each and every breath. I would die a thousand deaths to keep you safe because I love you too."

"Stupid, reckless dragon." Her arms slithered around his neck. Blackened water sluiced down his chest in dark little rivers.

It took three changes of the water to get them both clean. Burne carried her, still dripping wet, straight from the bath to the bed. Her back had scarcely touched the mattress before he was inside her. He was achingly gentle, moving against her in soft waves. Sophia knew he was frightened of hurting her, but she could feel the frantic need building inside of him. The pressure clenched his chest, held every one of his muscles rigid. This was how he would anchor himself in peace, how he would bury the rage that consumed him like fire every moment that they were apart.

Sophia understood how he needed it. She needed it too. She needed to be filled with him, to lose herself in the frenzy of want and release. It felt as if the world would somehow be righted if only she could hear him snarl out her name in climax.

"I've never been fragile before. Don't treat me as if I am now."

Burne brushed his thumb beneath her bottom lip. "I'll lose my mind if I hurt you."

"I'll lose mine if you don't fuck me the way a queen deserves to be fucked."

He loosed a growl, slamming into her up to the hilt. Sophia cried out, gripping him with her legs and urging him on. His retreat was torturously slow, dragging through her wetness until the tip of him was barely seated inside of her. Then he slammed into her again, so wildly that the bedframe groaned. Again and again he drew out and thrust back into her, his pace gaining momentum until he was feverishly pounding into her.

Fire.

Sophia was on fire. Molten pleasure pumped through her veins, travelling down and down until it pulsed between her legs. Just when she thought she couldn't take anymore, that her body would become ash, Burne pressed his thumb on that sweet spot between her thighs. She screamed, uncaring about who was returning to the castle to hear orgasm shattering her to pieces. Burne answered her climactic cry with a roar that made the room quake. On the grounds below, people were probably scurrying for cover as they feared the return of the dragon.

She was never going to catch her breath. Burne rolled them and she splayed across his chest, lifting and falling each time he gasped for air. The last droplets of water mingled with sweat, trickling between her breasts and down her forehead as the heat from him engulfed her.

Sophia was on a fire, but it didn't burn her. Instead, it climbed beneath her skin, shimmering and sizzled all the way to her heart until it was aflame. She was a burning queen and she would see every evil that sought to harm her people turned to ash.

CHAPTER 27

SOPHIA

B URNE ONLY SLIPPED FROM inside her when two blushing
maids entered and quickly exited the chamber. She dressed herself hurriedly, then called for the maids to bring clothing for Burne.
Their giggles could be heard down the hallway as they rushed to do as
she asked.

Not long after, Sophia and Burne stood hand in hand outside her
father's chamber door. A healer was silent at his bedside, his expression
grim. The king wasn't merely convalescing from illness, the healer
explained as Sophia peered down at her sallow-faced father. He was
dying. Black veins bulged beneath the surface of his paper thin skin.
That, the healer explained, was a symptom of poison.

George poisoned his own father to speed up his ascension to the
throne.

In life, Sophia held little but hatred for her father and she was fairly
certain the sentiment was shared between them. In death, she would
show him a kindness she hadn't known herself capable of. Even evil
men deserved mercy, a finite chance at redemption.

"Sophia?" Her father coughed, spittle collecting on his lower lip.

Sophia dabbed at his mouth with a handkerchief, clutching his
hand with hers. "I'm here, father."

"I feared you were dead. Devoured."

"Then why did you give me to the dragon?" She had to know.

"George—" A rattling cough cut off his words. "George convinced me it was the best decision for our kingdom. He claimed he found my father's journals, found proof that the stories of the dragon brides were true. He thought—" More coughing. "He believed you would return with the dragon and he could slay it, saving Calos and becoming a king of legend as his grandfather was before him." Father squeezed her hand weakly. "Forgive me, my daughter. You were a stubborn, untamable woman and I thought you were a risk to your brother's reign."

"The throne was mine by birth, father. I was stubborn and untamable because a queen has to be."

He shocked the breath right out of her when he answered, "I know. It was always meant to be you. George...he's not fit. I should have seen it sooner." His blue eyes were glassy, barely focusing on her when he repeated, "Forgive me, daughter."

"I do, father. I do."

Behind her, Burne pressed comforting fingers into her shoulder. The king lifted his bleary gaze, noting Burne for the first time. Sophia never expected the bright smile that lit her father's face when she introduced Burne as her betrothed. They discussed the petty details of wedding planning for a time, father obviously distracting himself from what the healer said may be only hours away.

"George?" Father asked when there was a quiet spell. "Will he come to pray with me? My time is nearing, I can feel it."

George? She wanted to scream at him. *George did this to you! George murdered and destroyed!* But Sophia was suddenly overwhelmed with sympathy. Here was a king reduced to a tearful old man, his body deteriorating, organs betraying him as they processed the poison and dumped it into his bloodstream. He wasn't a particularly good father and he wasn't a particularly good king. That didn't mean he deserved to die with grief in his heart.

"He'll be here." She lied, smiling softly. "Close your eyes and rest, father. I'll wake you when he arrives."

Burne was a steady presence behind her until the end. He pressed a gentle kiss to the top of her head as Father took his final, rasping breath and the invisible arms of the Gods gathered up his soul, carrying it back to the heavens whence it came.

Burne left to retrieve the healer, giving her a moment to herself. Their duty was not only to the sick and wounded, but also to the dead. Healers washed and prepared each and every body brought to them, be they kings or beggars.

"I'm sorry, my love." Burne embraced her in the hall outside the door.

In one day, she'd lost her family. She'd become queen. One day was all it took to change the course of her fate forever.

"Today is the last day." Sophia inhaled deeply, preparing herself for what had to come next. "We will make it known that today is the last day Calos will feel grief."

CHAPTER 28

SOPHIA

THEY BURIED HER FATHER after a quiet ceremony the following day. Four days after that, Sophia was crowned queen of Calos. Three weeks later, she and Burne were wed, not in the temple, but among the grassy fields of the valley. Each and every citizen was in attendance, much to the courtier's dismay and disgust. They were seated at massive tables with no hierarchical order. Sophia was sure to track down the women who selflessly covered her with their threadbare clothes and seated them and their families with herself and Burne.

Not a single one of their eyes were dry when she gifted them each new gowns, shawls, aprons, and whatever else they were in need of.

"A symbol," she told them. "Of all the prosperity to come. People will look to you and see hope."

The celebration was reminiscent of the festivals Calos hosted before her father deemed them frivolous and a waste of wealth. As king and queen, Sophia and Burne made it their directive to ensure no holiday went without joyous festivities.

Word was sent to each of the neighboring kingdoms, announcing the death of her father and their recent nuptials. Sophia was standing at the window of her chamber, reading another boring letter of congratulations from some lord or merchant when that creeping nausea climbed up her throat for the sixth time that morning. She covered her mouth, rushing for the waste barrel the maids had taken to leaving by her bed and emptying the scant breakfast she'd eaten.

Between her coronation and wedding, she hadn't given much thought to her mysterious illness. Gowns fit looser than they should and Burne had a dark crease of worry shadowing his brow when he looked at her. She imagined the stress from the previous two months was enough to make any woman sick.

Alas, she was a queen now and she couldn't afford to be unwell. The healer, a portly man with a kind face and rosy cheeks, took one look at her and grinned. Sophia was pleased with his ease around her, smiling back.

"My Queen." He dipped his head in a subtle bow. "You're not in need of me."

"I am. I've been sick for weeks. I can't keep more than a mouthful down. Is there a tonic I can drink? An herb, perhaps? It's very distracting."

He laughed, counting something out on his fingers. "If my math is correct, you'll feel better soon."

Sophia frowned. "I don't understand."

"The only question," He went on. "Is if the little one will come out with wings and fangs. I don't suppose you'll lay an egg…"

"An egg?" And then she understood. Her head felt light and before she could stop herself, Sophia sat right there on the stone floor. "I'm with child? How can you be so sure? You haven't even looked at me!"

"I've done this long enough to recognize the look in your eyes, your highness."

Silently, she searched her mind for the last time she remembered bleeding. It was…well it was before she met Burne.

Pregnant. She was pregnant. Sophia was going to have Burne's child.

The pounding of her heart became thunderous, drowning out whatever else the healer had to say. They both started as the chamber door flew open, Burne panting in the doorway with eyes of molten gold. He blinked rapidly, trying to disguise the color change, but it was too late. The healer saw and looked not one bit shocked. Perhaps Burne's secret wasn't as secret as they thought.

"Sophia? Are you alright?" He turned a vicious look on the healer.

She rushed to calm him, raising both hands and smiling sheepishly. "I've been feeling lightheaded and ill again, so I called a healer. I'm fine now."

"I'll give you two some privacy. Your highness," The healer bowed to Burne, giving him a wide berth as he exited and closed the door behind him.

"Why are you on the floor? Did you faint?"

"Nearly."

"What did the healer say? Are you unwell? Do you need medicine? Herbs? Tell me and I'll get them for you." Burne's eyes were brown again, wide and fearful. It was then Sophia remembered his mother, how often she was sick and bedridden. Panic pulled wildly in the bond between them.

She took his face in her hands, kissing him softly. "I'm not sick, Burne."

"Then what's wrong?"

Sophia took his calloused hand and brought it down to her lower belly. "We're going to have a child."

Burne dropped to the floor beside her, mouth agape. "A child?"

"Don't act so surprised. We've been very busy."

"A child." He repeated.

"I'm not going to lay an egg, am I?"

Humor and color returned to his face. "Oh, yes. Did I forget to tell you that part? You'll have to build a nest and sit in it every day for weeks."

"Oaf." She smacked his arm.

"Dragon." He corrected.

"Pretty lizard." She countered.

"So long as I am your lizard."

Hello my lovely reader! You made it to the end of Blood Feud! While your brain is all fluffed you with that happily-ever-after dopamine high, I have a favor to ask you. Could you hop over to Amazon (or scroll to the end of the book on your kindle) and leave a review? Reviews make the world go round for indie authors. Thank you for your kindness!

If you're ready for more comfy, standalone fated mates binge reads to fill your free hours then head over to the rest of the Dragon Brides series.

Let's stay in touch! Get updates when new books are released, get entered in signed book giveaways, and be the first to get your hands on review copies of my latest work by joining my newsletter.

A SNEAK PEEK AT BLACK HEART

D READ TICKLED UP FROM the base of her spine, settling on her nape and making the fine hairs there tingle. Mara had the unmistakable feeling she was being watched. Watched the way her father's miserable tiger watched her, a hungry creature ready to wait an eternity if it meant that one chance to strike.

She wasn't alone in the Blackwood, and whatever was with her was drawing nearer.

Mara sensed more than heard the parting of shrubs and ferns to her right. There was constant movement from the shadows of trees as their branches swayed in the whisper of autumn's cool breath. That inky dance made it nearly impossible to tell who or what was there. But it *was* there.

A hiss sounded from directly in front of her, a sharp exhale that became barely visible steam. Hot breath. Very hot, because the cloud was thick as smoke and triple the size of the small puffs leaving Mara's own mouth.

Another hiss of steam and the shadows suddenly coalesced, shifting until they took the unmistakable form of a beast. A long, serpentine body stretched from the cover of the trees; delicate wings tucked neatly along it. The thick legs that dropped down between those wings were muscled and armed at the base with claws that could easily tear through leather. Mara tracked along those onyx scales, taking in every lethal inch of dragon until she reached his head.

Compared to the dragon she'd caught a glimpse of earlier tonight, this one was small. Small was a relative term when it came to dragons, of course, because his presence still loomed over her the way only a predator could. Cat-like eyes glowed a brilliant green, two emeralds seated in the same infinite black that made up the night sky. Beautiful, mesmerizing gems that saw everything from the tears in her gown to the trembling thump of the pulse point on her jugular.

His head was rather cat like too; a pointed nose, diamond shaped features, what was likely horns taking place where triangular ears would be on a feline. Mara was struck with a strangely calming thought. If this was how she died, she would be glad. Not to be dead, but to be witness to such otherworldly beauty up close. It was the first and only time in her life where she was truly awestruck.

How treacherous and terrible beauty could be.

"I am honored to see you." She told the Beast of the Blackwood. "The stories do justice only to your violent deeds, not your divine beauty."

He blinked in response, nostrils flaring as another of those hissing breaths left him. It sounded rather like the bellows of a forge as they were pumped up and down.

Mara lifted her hand, hoping to still him for one more heartbeat, two if she were exceptionally lucky. She took in a great breath of her own, memorizing every flavor of autumn in the air. The wet sweetness of decaying leaves, the clean sting of cool air—the hot charcoal scent of dragon. Charcoal and wild ginger and warmth, if it had a scent.

"Let it be known that I died with my wings spread." She prayed to the Gods above her, the Gods she would soon spend her eternity serving in the heavens. "Let me be remembered as a bird uncaged."

The dragon moved lightning fast, as if he'd been giving her a chance to say her final words before making a meal of her. Rather thoughtful for a murderous beast.

A blistering hand wrapped around her waist, the tips of claws pressing threateningly into her flesh. Another hand reached out to grip her. Unable to watch her own end coming at her, Mara squeezed her eyes shut.

She didn't see the thick muscles in his back legs tense. She wasn't prepared when those legs exploded upwards, pushing through the canopy of the trees. The whoosh of broad wings opening to beat violently at the air finally drew her lids back. When she looked, all she saw was the vast starry expanse of night. Nothing above her. Nothing below her.

Mara screamed.

ALSO BY MOIRA KANE

Dragon Brides Series

A world once ruled by a noble race of dragons has fallen into the hands of the most powerful men. Fueled by greed, lust, and all manner of wickedness, the kings of Svalta start wars in their name, sending their sons to die and marrying their daughters off to those with enough wealth to fuel their drive for power. Lady Fate as other plans for the realm, her hand shifting the future for all when the first dragon bride in over a decade is taken in Calos.

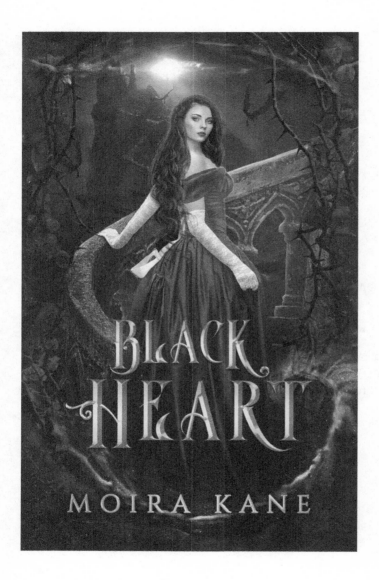

The story of a beauty and a beast reimagined.

Mara never dreamed of escape. Not really. How can a bird caged all her life ever think to fly? When a chance opportunity presents itself for the princess of Dunhill to flee her upcoming marriage and the cruel family that arranged it, she spreads her wings. But fate has other plans.

After narrowly surviving an encounter with the fabled Beast of the Blackwood—a dragon that stalks the forest that separates Dunhill from neighboring kingdoms—she finds herself in the unwilling company of Baron Gannon Black. He is mercurial at best, downright rude at worst.

The Black estate is teeming with secrets and the brusque baron is none too keen for Mara to unravel the mystery of the Black line. But hiding himself from the princess becomes impossible as he learns she is much more than the timid, bland daughter of the king. Can he keep her cloaked from the family that seeks to drag her back to her prison of etiquette and expectation or will her presence bring the long kept secrets of the Black family to light?

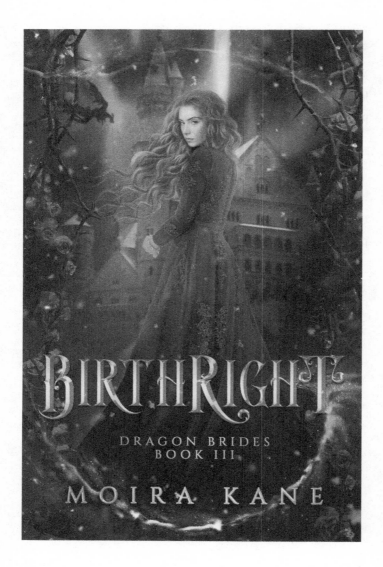

You cannot escape the fate you're born into.

Viggo abandoned his birthright and fled the demands of his father to live a simple life. He wanted for nothing in his quiet sanctuary in the Winter Wilds. It was easy for a dragon shifter to live among wild things. Here he was king, and he didn't have to care what anyone thought of him.

Everything changed when *she* appeared out of the forest like a walking dream, half-frozen and offering herself up as a bride.

Eleanor was as unrefined as a woman could be, bold and outspoken and so very different than the women at court. But years of isolation had made Viggo selfish and stubborn.

When Eleanor is revealed to be much more than a common maid, Viggo is forced to choose. Will he keep his quiet life, eternally alone, or will he step back into his father's world and face his past?

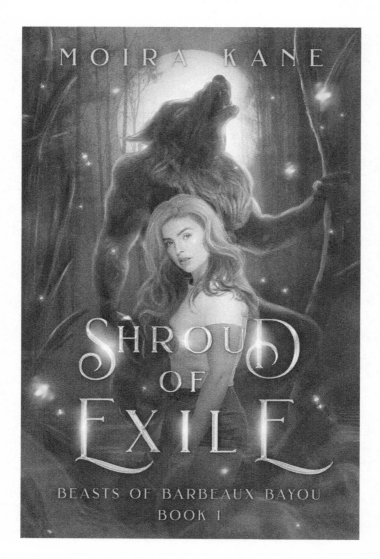

When Cady's boss unexpectedly died, she thought the worst that would happen to her was extra paperwork. Instead, she ended up stuffed in a trunk, driving down a no-name road in the middle of the bayou with two thugs that want their stolen money.

Just as she's about to become gator food, Cady is rescued by one of the notorious Barbeaux boys.

As Cady and Eli Barbeaux join forces to find out exactly who is looking for this missing money and putting them both in danger, they realize their lives are becoming entangled by more than an unsolved mystery.

But the bayou is full of secrets and Eli is supposed to keep them.

The Barbeaux line is old—ancient. Eli and his brothers are the last living descendants of *The Beast of Gévaudan*. Time isn't kind to those with preternaturally long lives and the burden of that violent family history is slowly killing them.

Now Eli has been given a second chance at living, but only if he can figure out who is after Cady and protect her from the fallout of bonding with a beast.

ABOUT THE AUTHOR

Raised in the picturesque Cascade mountain range, Moira is a born adventurer. She takes her inspiration from her surroundings, dreaming up dragons and warrior princesses as she scales treacherous mountain trails. When not writing, Moira is often found searching the woods for her reclusive husband and reading books with very happy endings.

Blood Feud is her debut novel, the first in the Dragon Bride series.

Instagram: @moirawritesromance

TikTok: @moirawritesromance

Join my newsletter here:

Made in United States
North Haven, CT
26 May 2024

52951339R00125